Sculpture of Grace

Olwyn Harris
Reading Stones Publishing

Stock image provided by Shutterstock: www.shutterstock.com
Cover models are AI generated images courtesy of Canva.com
Published by: Reading Stones Publishing
Helen Brown; and Wendy Wood
Cover Design: Wendiilou Designs
                Wendy Brown

For more copies contact the publisher at:
Glenburnie Homestead
212 Glenburnie Road
ROB ROY NSW 2360
Mobile: 0422 577 663

Email: Readingstonespublishing@gmail.com

To Trish, who has invested so much into the sculpture of my life, praying, and walking with me through all sorts of times...

Shipman Downs

1896

Rachel was lovely in form, and beautiful.
Jacob was in love with Rachel
and said, "I'll work for you seven years
in return for your younger daughter Rachel."

(Genesis 29:17-18)

"Rachel?" His eyes scanned the shed, past Smithy Jac shoeing his daughter's horse, into the shadows. Where was she? He would have guaranteed her inclination for Smithy Jac's blacksmithing workshop would mean she was around here somewhere. "Rachel!"

"Yes, Father... just having Blaze attended to."

She stayed hidden, but he sighed with relief. "Well, you don't need to supervise. Smithy has her in hand. You are needed in the house."

There was a pause. "Yes Father. Tell Mother I will be up shortly."

"No. She needs you there now. Our visitors have arrived earlier than expected. Rachel! I am serious. You must come now!"

There was another pause. "Yes, Father..."

He didn't move. "Now!"

The quiet tapping of hoof pick stopped. Smithy, who to this point had not faulted in the rhythm of his work, put down the horse's hoof and stood up. And turned around.

"Rachel!"

She grinned bashfully and swiped her unruly red hair out of her eyes, bumping the brim of her hat just a little higher with the handle of the hoof pick still in her hand. The ties on her long leather apron were wrapped around her middle, and her trousers were tucked into her boots. "Oh. Good afternoon, Father. Actually, I did need to supervise. Smithy Jac is not here."

"Oh, my Girl! What would your mother say? She is quite distraught because you can't be found! She wants you in the house... looking like a Leybourne lady, and not the farrier's lackey."

"I will... I will. When have I ever let you down? Please, stall her for half an hour... and her lady will be presented. It is fashionable to be just a little bit tardy."

"And you are wearing men's trousers! Again?" He sighed. "Really, Rachel, I don't need to remind you *that* is not fashionable... nor is being late. It is nerve-wracking. Please!"

"I said I will... so I will. And, Father, thank you..."

"Thank you?"

"For not saying I should be more like Leah."

"Your sister is covering for you. As am I. Now put Blaze in her stall, stop vexing your mother, and present yourself. In a skirt!"

He turned on his heel and walked quickly back to the house. Rachel returned her horse to the stables, running her hand along her roan coat with affection. She came back to the blacksmithing shed and took off the heavy leather apron and hung it on a wall rack that had been constructed from cast-off horseshoes. She turned around and was faced with the amused look of a man leaning against a post near the door. "Oh! And you are...?" she asked in surprise.

He took his hat from his head and ran his hand through a mop of dark red hair. "My name is Cob, Ma'am. Smithy's nephew. He collected me from town this afternoon."

"Huh. Hence why he could not be found. How long have you been standing there?"

"Long enough to see you know how to handle a hoof pick and a horse... and your father," he said with a charming twinkle in his eye.

She looked at him curiously. His chin was tilted, and he had a relaxed sort of manner about him. "You don't judge me for that. That's refreshing."

"Us red-heads need to stick together," he said with a grin that matched the amusement in his eyes. "I'm not going to presume Mrs Leybourne will be as accommodating. Aren't you expected to be somewhere, Miss Rachel?"

"Oh! Yes. Mother! Poor Billie will be beside herself." Cob's grin widened as she tossed her hat onto the rack, and it landed on the hook with a twirl. She quickly washed the grime off her hands in a bucket, drying them on a rag hanging on a nail. "Wish me luck. This is always an agonising trial. My cousins feel obligated to do an annual pilgrimage to their outlying relatives. We apparently need their world-weary expertise to inform and advance our country witlessness. They hate being here, matched only by my loathing of them bothering to come. It would be more civil to leave us alone. Last year Aunt Dorothea fixated on me as her particular project for special improvement. Obviously, she failed," she said with a chuckle as she indicated her trousers and boots.

He nodded. "Sounds like you have your work cut out for you... if you are to remedy your attire and your patience in such a short time."

"Oh. Yes. I am required in the drawing room." She swept back her hair that had fallen lose and tucked it behind her ears. "And already I am completely bored."

"Good luck..." he said with a nod as she rushed past him, disappearing through the door, running across the courtyard to the back of the house. Smithy Jac appeared at the door and looked at Cob staring after her.

"Oh no, son... no. That is not a good idea. Not at all. You cannot tilt your hat in that direction. Don't start something that cannot be finished, Cob. It would only end in a busted heart. Either yours, or hers, or both. That is a guaranteed dead end."

"I never started anything," said Cob with a shrug. He bent down and picked up his swag. Smithy indicated the ladder that led to the loft over the workshop that had been allocated as his quarters. "Wouldn't be game," he said with a smile as he effortlessly climbed the ladder.

⁕

2

Rachel poked her head through the service entrance and caught sight of Wilhelmina's familiar apron. "Pstt! Billie! Is the coast clear?"

"Miss Rachel! Thank goodness! Your mother is coming in every three seconds checking for you. Quick – they are all in the drawing room. Your Aunt Dorothea has been harping on about when you will be coming down. Get up those stairs, and I will be up shortly to help. Your dress is laid out on your bed: the green one."

"Oh grief. I feel like a Christmas tree in that thing. Red hair in a green dress is a terrible combination. And yet they insist."

"Your mother's choice. She said Dorothea made particular mention of it last visit; said it was 'flattering'. Go now, Honey," she pleaded with a whisper.

Rachel disappeared around the corner and could hear Billie giving her mother convoluted excuses as to why Rachel might not be found. She bounded up the stairs two at a time, pushed open the door and stared for a moment at the voluminous dress lying like a green swamp on her bed. She took a deep breath and started to unbutton her blouse. She poured some water into the basin and quickly washed her face and arms. Billie opened the door, then closed it behind her and turned the latch.

"Oh, Rachel, Honey. You haven't even taken off your trousers or boots yet. Quickly!"

"I don't have time. I'll just stick this over the top. No one sees my boots anyway."

"Are you sure?"

"More important to be prompt, I think. Here. Help me get into this thing."

"You are past any chance of prompt. Stand still while I button the back." She picked up the button hook and quickly worked down the buttons. "Drench yourself in lavender water. Leave your hair down. It is your flattering feature. We will add this pretty little shawl, and no one will notice... perhaps."

"Do I have to wear the shawl?"

"I think it will cover a multitude of sins, Honey. Lateness being the first."

Rachel rolled her eyes as Billie dabbed some lip-colour, smeared some powder on her nose and pinched her cheeks. "Just smile, Honey, and Aunt Dorothea will soon forgive your tardiness. You could confess to reading a gripping novel... or being engrossed in the needlepoint details of some fancy-work project."

Rachel groaned and gave Billie a grateful hug and braced herself for the affliction to come, pasted on a smile and descended the staircase at a casual pace.

Her mother turned and saw her. "Rachel! Where have you... no matter. Dorothea has already started. Look attentive. Come," her mother said as she picked up a stray novel that was lying on the sideboard in the hall. She guided Rachel through the door with a glorious smile, holding the book as evidence. "Look who I found wandering the hallways reading a book? She lost track of time..."

Rachel went over and offered her aunt the obligatory welcome kiss. "Hello, Aunt Dorothea. How wonderful to see you again. It doesn't feel like a year already."

"That is because it is not yet a year, Rachel my dear. We came last year in October. It is only now early May."

"Surprising, isn't it, how time marches on. Oh! My cousins have joined us again. Felix, Gwendolyn.... welcome back to Shipman Downs. Oh. And you've brought a friend. How... intriguing. A friend."

Aunt Dorothea bustled to her side and lowered her voice in whispered tones. "Yes, Rachel my dear, that is Walter. Walter's parents are dear friends who are most deliciously positioned, and they are also on very good terms with Gwendolyn's fiancé's family. Since she is engaged, this will most likely be the last year that Gwendolyn will be joining us in the country," she said quietly. "It is so appropriate that Walter could come with us since he is interested in learning about pastoral responsibilities. And that is why our visit is earlier this year. Walter is going to stay for a period... and fall under the excellent supervision and tutelage of your father. What an adventure this will be for him."

Rachel eyed Walter warily. He stood, bored and unimpressed, with a drink in his hand looking at a painting on the wall. It was evident his enthusiasm for the scope of his adventure was not matched by Aunt Dorothea's fervour. Aunt Dorothea went over and tugged his sleeve. "Come, Walter, I want you to meet Rachel." He turned and stopped short as he caught sight of her green gown, her red hair tumbling over her shoulders, and her soft shawl that had slipped to rest in her crook of her elbows. He raised his brow and smiled.

"So, *this* is Rachel. How delighted I am to meet you at last. Aunt Dorothea has told me so much about you."

"Has she? Funnily enough, I didn't even know you existed. And have you met Leah? My sister." Rachel grabbed at her sister's arm and pushed her forward. "She painted the picture you are gazing at. It has been critiqued as a very accomplished piece."

His eyes never left Rachel's face. He didn't acknowledge Leah or her painting. "We met earlier," he said dismissively. "Where have *you* been hiding?"

"Oh, well... you may not have heard. My mother said she caught me reading a book."

"Reading? So, you are a scholar? What subjects do you enjoy?"

"You know, I am dying for a drink. Leah will tell you more about her painting. Bowls of roses are an endless source of inspiration. She reads books as well. I will be back in a tick."

"Let me get..." he started after her to offer his assistance.

She stopped and arrested his attempt to follow. "No need, Mr.... Walter. I can manage." And she bolted to the sideboard and poured a glass of lemon water. This was ridiculous. She closed her eyes and wondered how she could escape.

Her mother came over and stood close by her side. "What do you think of our visitors, Rachel, joining us again so soon? Isn't this lovely?"

"I think what I always think. It is an enormous intrusion, and I can't wait for them to leave."

Mother continued without any acknowledgement of Rachel's pout. "I am hoping that because they have been able to come earlier, perhaps they may stay longer than their usual month. And what about Walter? What do you think about him?"

"I think he looks about as enamoured with all of this carry-on as I am. He is spoilt and bored. I doubt he will stay."

"Oh, he will stay. Dorothea has intimated that he has been required to complete three tasks for him to inherit. He has already attended to a period on a merchant ship, and now there is to be a season on a farm. We are honoured with the good fortune to accommodate him for this task."

Rachel stared at her and for one horrifying moment she thought her mother was going to jump up and down, clap her hands whilst chortling 'Goodie!'. "Huh. So, what is the third challenge? Trekking through the jungles of the Amazon basin?"

"Dorothea said that the next obligation will only be revealed part way through the completion of the current one. She said she will keep me abreast of the situation, so we know how to support him appropriately."

Rachel rolled her eyes. "Really, Mother? Why are you so intent on helping a spoilt brat like him? He doesn't belong here. How long is this prescribed visit? A fortnight?" She groaned at another possibility. "Surely, he will not remain here for the entire duration of Aunt Dorothea's stay. They generally stay for weeks!"

"Oh no, Rachel, you completely misunderstand me. He is staying for at least six months. These assignments are taking a full year in the execution of them."

She looked over and watched him tapping his fingers out of tedium on his glass. Leah was smiling eagerly whenever he muttered a monosyllabic response to her attempts at conversation. "Six months! That is ludicrous. He doesn't want to be here. What can he possibly hope to achieve in six months?"

Her mother smiled serenely and picked up her glass, murmuring as she walked away, "I anticipate that a great deal can be accomplished in six months." Then she herded everyone into the dining room for dinner.

3

"I think I have caught you out, Miss Rachel."

Rachel spun around from the verandah rail where she was leaning, the material in her green dress, snagging on the wooden rail as she turned. She saw the scuffed toe of her boot exposed and she quickly pulled it back into hiding under the hem of her skirt. "You probably have. What do you suppose you have caught me at?"

"Plotting an escape. Ever since you have arrived this evening you have been scheming your escape from Dorothea's clutches. And now you have managed it. You are taking some respite of fresh night air and cool May breezes."

"Well, Walter, it seems you pride yourself on perceptive insights. And perhaps you may be right." She looked at him and felt an unaccountable groan develop in the pit of her stomach. It was all she could do to keep it supressed. He was so confident he had nailed the summary of her predicament so accurately. In fact, he had missed it by a mile. This little dally on the verandah was not the destination of her escape... but the launch of it. And inconveniently, he had interrupted her.

He took her observation as a compliment, and smiled, encouraged. "I do think I hold a level of insight." He came over and joined her by the rail. "I can offer a couple of reflections that may amuse you," he said.

Rachel considered him and wondered how to unlatch his apparent growing attachment to her. "I doubt you can tell me anything I don't already know, as I have greater experience of the people in the drawing room than yourself."

"Ahh. We will see. Take Aunt Dorothea. She is a lady who considers an excellent social station to be the highest attainable virtue. So that makes me very virtuous in her eyes. She is seduced by the idea that I am to inherit a fortune and considers that your family could do with the social buffing that rubbing shoulders with her family... and my family, will offer. You see, it is my observation that she wants to upgrade you to more acceptable social levels. I am the tool in her hand to hone her prowess in this project."

"You? You think *you* are the tool of choice for my redemption? You are not shy, Mr..."

"Lincroft. Walter Lincroft. At your service." And of course, he offered a bow.

"...you are not shy, Mr Lincroft. I wonder that you would dare to show such boldness on the first evening of a visit. It is an extreme form of presumption and very forward of you."

"I do not say it to be forward..."

Rachel laughed. "Oh, but I think you do."

"No. No, not at all. You see, I have developed an understanding of the situation I find myself in. This is a game that cannot be overturned. The cards have been dealt and my participation is determined. So instead of refusing to play my hand, I have resolved to partake in the exercise with insight and cleverness. And then, by doing that, both parties get what they want. I don't want to disappoint my uncle, nor do I want to offend Aunt Dorothea, but I also need to secure the achievement of my goals."

Rachel considered his eager eyes in the shadows of the evening. So, there might be more to Walter Lincroft than tapping his bored fingers, tedious conversation, and polite social courtesies. "And what are your goals, Mr Lincroft?"

"To inherit. That's number one. My uncle has laid down some very specific requirements for this to proceed. Inconvenient no less. But he seems to think my heritage and linage are not sufficient. Two... why not find a way to fulfil these necessary obligations with the least amount of pain and suffering, and to enjoy myself in the process? So, you see, Miss Rachel... I think I could well be the means for your escape; and you are the means for mine. You see, mutually – we are both tools to hone and sharpen each other's lives."

"This is really what you think? So, the charge of presumption stands confirmed. It seems my insight was no less perceptive than your own."

"Perhaps. But my insight considers that you are irked by your life here, you are underestimated, and you are destined for greater things."

She laughed. And it rang out over the courtyard like a beautiful bell tolling. "You may be right about that. I am definitely irked. But I don't think you are the greater things that I am destined for, Mr Lincroft."

"Please don't be too quick to dismiss me. I am not so shabby that I cannot amuse and entertain if you would give me a try."

"Give you a try? How can I 'give you a try' like I might try on a hat to see if it matches my outfit?"

"But that is exactly what I am suggesting. Try it on. See how it fits. This is my way of making the intolerable bearable. I think you will be amused at how we could complement each other for the duration of my time here."

How could he expect her to 'try him on' and then in the next breath declare her home intolerable? Rachel smiled elegantly to cover her disgust. "Ahh. Amusement. For the duration of your internment at Shipman Downs. I don't recall you mentioning that my company was part of the obligations required of you."

"Exactly. I would be very much obliged if you would consider easing my pain... just a little." His charm and his fortune were a combination that meant Walter always had doors opened for him. Without exception. He was not at all disturbed by Rachel's reluctance. It just added a sprinkling of interest to the tedium of his quest.

Rachel considered him the vainest of men she had ever encountered. The inconvenience of his suggestion did not tempt her to accommodate alleviating his type of world-weariness that is generally only an affliction of the indulged. "Well, Mr Lincroft, I think I am required inside. If you will excuse me?"

"Miss Rachel?" She turned back, her skirt swishing elegantly as she paused while he nodded towards her. "I will convince you otherwise. You will see that what I propose is completely reasonable."

"Oh grief, Mr Lincroft. If you think that is flattering, you have obviously been reduced to the social circles of the extremely bored and tedious. I am not tempted to change my routines just to humour your lack of distracting pastimes. You may have to find other ways to help you survive the onerous obligations that your privilege expects of you."

He smiled undeterred. "I respect an honest assessment. You have been honest with me, Miss Rachel."

"All to no avail it would seem. Good night, Mr Lincroft." If her scheming for escape in one direction was thwarted, she could feign fatigue and pursue escape another way.

She turned inside and any efforts he made to detain her further were futile. Rachel found Leah and proceeded to convince her it was an entirely good plan for them to retire together. Without delay. "Come up with me. We've been here long enough," Rachel cajoled.

"Rachel, please. I am enjoying myself. Can't I be left alone to do what amuses me sometimes too?"

But Rachel was immune to Leah's pleas to be left to enjoy their company a little longer. "If we leave together, it will not be considered ill-mannered. I have a headache that is truly annoying me."

"Humph! You are the annoying one. Your fictitious headaches are familiar to me," Leah said, looking wistfully at her cousins deep in an amusing story.

"But acceptable to everyone else present."

"Very well. But you owe me."

They made their apologies and walked up the stairs together. In their room, they helped each other with the process of disrobing. Leah adjusted her eyeglasses as she stared horrified at Rachel's trousers and boots that she was still wearing as she stepped out of her petticoat. They were smeared with dust and grime. "You weren't actually wearing these inside all evening Rachel?" she cried. "That is just embarrassing! What if someone caught you?"

"Well, no one is going to be looking under my skirt. People are too interested in smiles and shawls to worry about hems and boots."

"You risked Mother being shamed in front of her sister. Rachel you should take more care! They are our relatives, and their company should be respected."

"Well, she wasn't embarrassed, and it is part of the entertainment for me to see what I can get away with, regardless of the proliferation of petticoats and skirts. So, tell me, what is your plan to survive the next month with our condescending and cantankerous cousins?"

"What do you mean?" she asked, as Rachel helped unlace the bodice of her corset. "Unlike you Rachel, I do actually enjoy visiting with my cousins and Aunt Dorothea."

"Oh Leah. You can't mean that. They are all snobs. Gwendolyn is absolutely incapable of talking about anything other than her upcoming marriage. I really don't know what sort of pleasure you can derive from their company."

"They have stories aplenty of society and culture and the fine arts. It is something we never see here. It is a pleasant distraction."

"As long as it is always connected to Gwendolyn and her wedding. How can you find her incessantly mind-numbing choice of topic remotely distracting?"

Leah shook her head. "I expect we will be invited to the wedding. And I do appreciate the feminine flair required to organise such a refined event... which is nothing like your grossly inappropriate forge-work. Just leave me to enjoy their company. I have been looking forward to their next visit since they left."

"Don't insult my forge-work, and I won't insult your tedious inclination for society!"

"Come on, Rachel, that is the least lady-like thing that has ever entered your head to do. And there have been plenty of contestants for that prize over the years. Being a tom-boy when you are nine is endearing. Now it is disturbing."

"Leah! I have never asked you to approve of it. I like creating this way. It is such a powerful medium. It beats pastel paints, or soft cotton threads, or fine china plates filled with morning tea any day."

"But it is not a feminine past time! If mother knew you were still pursuing this, you know she would shut it down."

"You're not going to tell her, are you? Please, Leah, you promised." Rachel looked at Leah as she brushed out her hair. Leah's hair was red like her sister's, but limper, thinner, duller. It never attracted the compliments that Rachel received.

"Well, like I said, what was tolerable when you were younger, is no longer appropriate. You should have outgrown it."

"How can you outgrow passion? What you ask is impossible."

"Oh grief. You make it sound like some wild romantic love affair. Well, it is not. It is an infatuation with delusion."

"But it is that exactly – this is the one thing that makes me feel truly alive. This infatuation, as you call it, is not delusion, nor just a passing fancy... it is the way that I can make sense of my life. Surely that is what passion is!"

"It is actually playing like a child in coal dust and grime. You know it is not possible for such a thing to bypass discovery much longer. It has even outlasted Billie's projections. I will give you credit for your ingenuity in keeping it hidden though. But ultimately, you will do just the same as me when it comes down to it... and you will marry who you are told to marry."

"Not if I can help it."

"Well, I suspect Mother and Aunt Dorothea are going to challenge your defiance on that. They were determined to ensure you and the eligible young Walter were thrown together continually all evening."

Rachel cringed. "Augh! Exactly my point. He is such a grebe."

"I assume that is intended to be derogatory and not a reference to the water duck. Grow up, Rachel. We are not in nursery school."

"How could you have a different opinion of Walter? I saw him brushing the crumbs off the tablecloth that spilt from the breadbasket. He thought we were so vulgar. It is so insulting the way he considers everything that is normal for us, is so completely beneath him."

"I think he is privileged and used to things a certain way. But he is handsome and amusing... and I like him."

"How? He is the most arrogant, spoilt specimen of indulged humanity that has ever come to visit! Mother says he is going to be here for six months!"

Leah paused and raised her eyebrows. "Is he now? Six months. Why?"

"Oh, I don't know... some sort of scheme that is part of his inheritance. I don't even care why! I care that he is actually here, and we have to endure the indignity of his self-importance for such an extended period."

"Walter tells such interesting stories. He went sailing on a merchant ship, and he told me about some of his adventures with the first mate. He saw some amazing things."

"Or... he saw ordinary things, and he up-sells them as astonishing to increase his pathetic quota of noteworthy qualities."

"Rachel, you have become so cynical! He was amusing and civil."

"I find him boorish and distasteful."

"But of course you do, Rachel. Because beautiful Rachel is always the one who is sought after for attention, and she can afford to have ridiculous scruples."

"Oh, that is rubbish! Rachel is the one who is always told to be more like her responsible older sister, because Leah alone knows how to behave like a true lady."

"Well, it wouldn't be difficult if you just took notice, Rachel. You insist on doing things your own way."

"Well too bad, because I happen to like being me, and I happen to like doing things in a way that reflects me."

Leah shook her head and climbed into bed. "Good night, Little Sister."

4·

Rachel paused at her dressing-room door, and then went back to her closet, grabbed a full skirt, and pulled it on over her trousers before she left. She knew all the spots where the floorboards creaked between her room and the back door, and Rachel avoided them skilfully as she tiptoed down the stairs. She had arranged with Smithy Jac to give her two hours... two early morning hours of access to the forge, so she could work on her projects. She had made all sorts of practical iron forged items under his tutorage: a hat-rack; a tack-rack; a boot-jack; a coat-rack... all with some creative twist. Then she started crafting a variety of garden ornaments... flowers, dragonflies, and butterflies, even a model windmill. She enjoyed making that piece as it was larger than the others, and she had spent the time reminiscing a childhood adventure that involved climbing ropes and a really grand view from the top. These iron novelties were made mostly out of small iron scraps and cast-off horse-shoes. But these little projects were only ever homework for what was to come. Now Rachel had it in her head that she was ready to try her first fully-fledged project. She had convinced her father that this would be something to stand at the main entrance of Shipman Downs... in honour of her grandfather, who had been a Midshipman in Her Majesty's Navy. When he discharged from Royal Service, he came here to farm, and their family never left. Her endeavour was to make an artwork of iron, a symbolic replica of a ship to honour the family's nautical history which inspired their property's name.

She told Smithy Jac in serious tones that this was her graduating assignment as an artist – her first real art commission. The concept drawings she had sketched in her books were something of a general guide rather than technical plans to follow. The dimensional space already existed in her mind, and she was filling in this mental picture with the iron from the forge. This project was much bigger than anything she had made before. She no longer could be confined to using cast off horseshoes, so she had been salvaging larger sections of metal from various implements from around the farms in the valley. She was thrilled by the way it was coming together, following lines, adding texture, and character, and interest. Smithy Jac was the only one who appreciated her obsession with iron work. The others who knew of her fascination with the medium were either confused, critical, or like her father, indulgently tolerant. But she refused to give in to their disparaging disapproval and her craftmanship went underground.

She pushed open the large, shed door in the dark crisp morning air, discarded her skirt, and tied her scarf around her hair, holding it back out of the way. She lit the lanterns around the workshop and donned her long leather apron. She fired up the forge and manoeuvred the trolley with her working frame, into the centre of the workshop. The large skeletal frame was hollow and bare, and today she was adding to the bow of the ship. She pulled on her leather gloves, dragged out the metal from her allocated stack and poked it into the glowing coals of the forge, pumping the bellows, and rotating the rod until it glowed red hot. Then she started. It was that first strike of the hammer that always seemed to jar. She could never get used to it. It was breaking the silence in her head. But once that first strike on the anvil reverberated out into the morning stillness, it was like the starting-gong of a wrestling match. She found herself stepping into an arena of rhythm and pace;

manoeuvring, defending, and attacking with a vital creativity that shut everything else out.

Cob jolted in his bunk. Uncle Jac was at the anvil already! Sleeping in was not a great way to start his first day. His head was cloudy with sleep as he pulled on his trousers and shirt in the dark and stumbled to the edge of the loft overlooking the workshop. What he saw shocked him wide awake. Under the light of lamps, and the glow of the forge, was the unmistakable figure of Rachel working, her mop of red hair tied back under a scarf. Her rhythm, her stance, her focus, her workmanship drew him into a mesmerising trance. He had no idea how long he sat on the ledge of the loft floor watching her.

"Morning, Miss Rachel! How is she coming along?" Smithy Jac's husky morning voice rang out as he came through the doorway, his white beard blurred in the familiar smoky haze of his tobacco pipe.

"Is that the time already? I feel like I've only just started."

"No. No. You're fine. Just keep going. I came over a bit earlier to show Cob around, grab him some breakfast, that sort of thing."

"Who?" she said distractedly staring at the angle of the rod in her hand.

"Cob. My nephew. He came in yesterday... from the train."

"Oh. Cob..." Suddenly, as if by instinct she glanced up at the loft and saw him sitting there... his legs dangling over the edge near the ladder. "How long have you been there?" she asked him directly.

"Long enough to see you know how to handle a hammer and iron tongs ... and a forge," he said with that same charming grin. "Good morning to you, Miss Rachel..." he added as he swung down the ladder. "Uncle Jac..." he acknowledged as his boots hit the floor in a puff of dust that lit up in the first streaks of morning light streaming through the door.

Smithy cocked his head at Cob in silent warning. "You come with me. We will leave Miss Rachel to her work as she still has some time before we start."

"She does?"

"Yes. She is *working*. One day she will have her own studio... but just at the moment... we share. So, we will be gentlemen and not disturb her."

"She didn't look disturbed for a second. Anything you need, Miss, that I can get for you?"

Rachel watched that exchange with a level of distraction. It felt odd to realise she had an audience... and for how long? Of course, if Cob was occupying the loft, realistically he would not have slept through the very first strike of her hammer. So, he may have been watching since she first arrived. Yet he didn't interrupt. He didn't offer an opinion. And he didn't draw attention to himself. Hmm. "Umm... need?"

"Yes. Is there anything I can get you when I go with Uncle Jac to grab breakfast? Have you eaten?"

"No. It is too early for me to eat yet. I have breakfast when I go back to the house. By then I am usually starving."

"Oh. Anything else then?"

"Hmm. A bucket of water from the well would be helpful."

"To drink or to dunk?"

"Both actually. Running low on both of those."

He nodded and grabbed two buckets and left. He returned shortly, both in hand. He put them down and left without comment. It was a while before Rachel looked up and saw the buckets had already been delivered – silently standing witness to her work, just like Cob had done earlier. Huh. How many men did she know who would do something without advertising their chivalrous contribution? She grabbed a pannikin down off the cup-rack that was another of her horseshoe constructions. She took a long, slow drink... soothing the rasping in the back of her throat. Then she went back to work. Time slowed to the rhythm of her striking and hammering, her attention totally focused on what was in front of her. Time became meaningless.

There was a tap on her shoulder, and she jolted. Cob was there with that constantly entertained look in his eye. He held her skirt in his hand, and he offered it to her. "You have a visitor..." he said indicating the front of the shed's open doors with a tilt of his chin.

She glanced in that direction and saw Walter looking around.

Rachel quickly retreated back into the shadows behind her work frame. She pushed her hammer into Cob's hand and grabbed her skirt from him; took off her leather apron and gloves, shoving them into his arms. She juggled the layers of skirt up over her trousers, buttoning it hurriedly. She took off her scarf, flicked out her hair and arranged the scarf around her shoulders. Cob indicated a smear of char across her cheek, and she rubbed at it with the heel of her hand and a corner of her scarf. Cob nodded as he wordlessly donned the apron in his hand, wrapping the cord deftly around his middle a couple of times. He smeared some char dust over his forehead, cleared his throat, and his eyes crinkled with a grin. "Yes, Ma'am. I think what you have suggested is perfectly doable," he said clearly and firmly.

Walter turned around and strode inside. "Miss Rachel! Leah said you would be down here somewhere. What are you doing out here... in a *shed*... so early? I thought we might have breakfast together."

"Oh. No thank you. I've already eaten. Although, thank you for thinking of me, Walter." She turned to Cob and nodded very officially. "Well done, Cob. This looks like it is going well. I think Father will approve of this progress," said Rachel formally.

He nodded seriously and handed her the hammer. Rachel juggled it awkwardly and eventually put it down. He pointed to the lines along the construction. "It is definitely a difficult project, but I am very pleased with the way it is coming together. I'm taking particular note of the principles of symmetry and surface texture, particularly through this section here. I trust you are happy with those."

"I am..." She looked into his face and nodded. He got it. He understood what she was doing. And that lit a light behind her eyes.

Walter cleared his throat and stared at the mangled ironwork, still very skeletal in its development. "Really? It is a frightful eyesore! Rachel you can't be pleased with this. I can't imagine your father would want your Blacksmith working on a project of this type. Smith, don't you have cartwheels to mend or something useful to attend to?"

"I do. Cartwheels a-plenty. We get to turn our hand to all sorts of trades. Blacksmith, farrier, wheelwright, and general roustabout. Even artisan. This project is a commission that Miss Rachel is supervising. I work on it before I start my hours. Nothing has been lost. And a great deal is gained." Cob stood up tall; his shoulders squared.

Walter's lip curled in disgust, and he turned back to Rachel. "It's a monstrosity! That's what it is. How is it even conceivable that your father would expect you to come into a blacksmith's workshop, at any time of day, but especially before breakfast is served. Such diligence, even from his daughter, is admirable... but only in small doses. After that it becomes common."

Cob raised his brow and noticed Rachel held onto the edge of the construction framework, until her knuckles blanched, and she stared at the ground silently. She was astonished that he would consider he was entitled to air his opinion so frankly, especially as a mere visitor. Were manners completely foreign to him? "Have you ever been to an art gallery, Walter?"

"Of course. I have access to many art galleries. Some are quite elite. A gallery visit is a pleasant enough social occasion. But again... only in small doses."

"Have you ever been to the studio that *makes* the art that hangs in the gallery?"

"I did a sitting once. But it was tedious... and dirty. Smelt like turpentine."

"Much like farming, which is also tedious and dirty. Whether the medium be a paddock, or oils, or masonry, or clay, or textiles, or ironwork... the raw work that creates the canvas, is rarely as clean as the finished article. I have no problem with the coaldust behind creating this piece... because without it, how could the balance and texture of the finished artwork ever be achieved?"

"That is all nonsense. But I guess, I could allow, for a lady, nonsense is completely permissible."

She tinkled a polite laugh, but Cob noticed her eyes were cold and angry. "Of course, we must be allowed to have our amusements. Come let us go." Rachel ushered him out of the shed, and then turned back and mouthed a grateful *'Thank you'* to Cob before she joined

Walter to walk back to the verandah of the house. Tears stung the back of her eyes in a furious rage as they walked side by side, and she benignly enquired after what activities the cousins had planned for the day.

5.

Leah sat with Gwendolyn after dinner on the lounge, discussing the embroidery she was working on. Aunt Dorothea had retired with a sore throat and one of Billie's lemon and ginger elixirs. Felix was reading a book; Walter sat comfortably at the card table shuffling the pack of cards. Rachel poured some wine into a glass and stared across the room with a type of detached surveillance. Gwendolyn was giving very specific advice about what fashionable stitches Leah should be using for her project, like the ones she was using on her wedding veil. Given that Leah's needlework was accomplished in every sense, Rachel was embarrassed by Gwendolyn's tone of superior expertise. Leah just smiled pleasantly and repeatedly tried to draw Walter into the discussion by asking for his opinion. But he ignored her efforts to be amiable and began dealing the cards, focused intently on the count.

Rachel noticed there had been a change from the Walter who had arrived little more than a week ago. In that short space of time, he no longer held a bored disdain of what these country cousins of Shipman Downs had to offer. Now his manner held the fraternal tone of being familiar. Walter chummied up to her father, rode the paddocks, asked discerning questions on matters that did not interest him, and smoked cigars with an air of congenial ease. To all accounts, Walter Lincroft had moved in. He had adopted the role of oldest son, in a household that only had two daughters. And the adults in the house were delighted by his silent take-over. Mr Leybourne was both relieved and elated to have such a willing protégé. Rachel shook her head at the horror of her revelation. But Leah did not notice, or if she did, she gave no indication that this bothered her in any way.

"Come, Rachel, sit at the table and make up the second pair. You can partner with me," said Walter.

"Felix can play. I have a headache, and my constitution is not strong enough for such activities this late in the evening."

Felix looked up from his book. "No thanks," he said indifferently.

Gwendolyn stood up and took her place at the card table, impatiently gesturing for Leah to take the seat beside her. "At home we always have an eventide social activity. My fiancé is always a willing partner. Such a diversion does not impede the routine of an early morning constitutional. The two activities are completely compatible if managed appropriately."

"Management, of course, is the difference," said Walter. "Rachel is up every morning even before the sparrows, and every morning I find her down in that grubby blacksmithing workshop supervising... whatever it is. You need to take better care of yourself Rachel."

Rachel ran her hand over her forehead and felt an internal scream light up her belly. "Goodnight then."

"Rachel! Where are you going? We want to play cards," said Gwendolyn with a pout.

"I am taking care of myself... as Walter suggested." She quickly left the room, but instead of taking the staircase, she ran out the back to the servants' rooms.

Billie was there attending to some mending. She looked up as Rachel came in, her face flushed indignantly. "Rachel... Honey... what is it?" she said, putting down her stitching.

"That... that..." Her voice faulted.

Rachel went over to Billie who quickly stood up and gave her a strong hug. "Slow it down, Honey. Slow it down," she said gently. Her breathing slowed and she took some deep breaths in time with Billie's gentle, generous bosom. "See... when you slow down and pause... you are able to think more clearly. Now, Honey... what is it that you need?"

"I need some space away from that suffocating drawing room! I'm going down to the stables. Blaze, at least, has some sense about her." And she ran from the house before Billie could say anything further.

Billie frowned and sat down quietly and picked up her mending. But she didn't immediately make any stiches. Instead, she prayed, and hedged Rachel in with the protection of God's angels.

⁕⁕⁕

Rachel ran across the courtyard glowing under the silver light of a full moon. There was no appreciation for its beauty tonight. It just added a sinister sheen to the cool night air.

She ran into the stable and pulled open Blaze's stall. Rachel fell on Blaze's neck and entwined her fingers through her mane. Tears dropped unheeded onto the hay under her hooves. Breathe. Breathe. Blaze stood quietly, patiently offering to carry the load of her mistress' distress. Rachel closed her eyes and buried her face in Blaze's mane. Slowly, she felt her breathing calm and her mind soothe, just like the way Billie had soothed her through a lifetime of storms. Rachel picked up Blaze's soft grooming brush and slid her fingers under the worn leather strap. Slowly, under the light of the moon streaming in through the shutters, she ran the brush along her neck and withers. Here, with Blaze, she didn't have to justify anything or explain. Here she could just be herself. How long she stood there she didn't know, and at first, she wasn't aware of the flicker of a lantern approach.

"Miss Rachel? Are you okay?"

She turned around. "Oh, Cob. No... I..." Tears, still wet on her cheeks, glistened in the lamp light that he held in his hand.

He stood there. Uncertain what to do. What happened to the confident, brash, focused Rachel he met when he first arrived? "Want to talk?"

"No. I want to ride... and I don't want to come back."

"Well, if it is a ride you want... I'm guessing that means I'm coming too. Given the time of night, I can't let you go alone. Where do you want to go?" He grabbed Blaze's bridle even as he said it.

"You aren't going to try and talk me out of it?"

"Do you want me to? I could. It just looks as though you really could do with some fresh air."

She hesitated for a moment, but when he bridled Blaze in her stall, blew out the lantern, and jumped up onto her bareback, she allowed him to pull her up behind him. "So... you tell me where you would like to be right now..." He walked the horse out past the courtyard and then cantered out along the track in the moonlight.

Rachel leant against his back, her arms around his waist. The rhythm of their ride moving and rocking and holding her. More calming. More soothing. "Take the left fork. I'll show you something," she said. When the moonlight faded as it hid behind some clouds, Cob slowed Blaze to a walk. And then, when the moon came out and he resumed their light canter under the silver wash that gently spread out over the paddocks.

They came up to a shed made out of traditional vertical timber slabs. Cob eased Rachel down from behind him, and then jumped to her side. He looked around. "What is this place?"

"This is where I come when I want to escape. It used to be attached to a Shepherd's hut in my grandfather's day. The hut burnt down in a bushfire that ran through the whole property... but the shed somehow escaped the fire. There was a whole mystery that happened here about twenty or so years ago. A kidnapping of four ladies... and they were held here for days. One of them was pregnant and her baby was born here before they were found and rescued."

Cob froze. He stared at the shed in the bright light of the full moon. Rachel stopped and watched his jaw work up and down.

"Cob? Are you okay?"

"This is the place where that baby was born? Here?"

"Yeah... it was quite the sensational story. Bushrangers; abduction; ransoms... and a newborn baby thrown into the mix. They were all safe in the end. Happy-ending I guess."

Cob swore and sat down on his haunches. "Here?" He swallowed.

"Cob, what's going on?"

"Rachel. I was that kid. This is where I was born. Theodore Jacob Ruben Horne – I'm the *kid* born in the barn while his mother was held hostage."

Rachel's eye flew wide open. "You? You were born here? How do you know that?"

"Mum told me the story of how she was taken at night. And before help came, she went into labour. My godmother was one of the other women. The interesting twist was that my godfather was accused of the kidnapping. They are all family to me. It was a standing joke in our family, that Jesus was born in a stable too."

"Is that why you came to Shipman Downs? Is this why you are here?"

"Well, no... but it has to be the same place. How many stories like that are around this valley? I knew I was born here in the valley and thought I might eventually come across it... but I'm not on a mission of self-discovery if that is what you mean."

"Why didn't Smithy Jac say anything?"

"Guess he never got around to mentioning it – him being a chatty type and all. He has other stuff on his mind just now anyhow."

"I like your uncle very much."

"I've got great memories of being Uncle Jac's offsider in his workshop as a kid. He is a master craftsman. Very experienced. He managed all the blacksmiths at the military compound for years. When he discharged, he took this job to stay off the map while they were sending troupes over to the war against the Boers in Africa. He just lay low and never left. Came up here because Mum knew the valley."

"He came to Shipman Downs to escape active duty?"

"Says he is past putting himself through that for someone else's fight."

"Not very patriotic..."

Cob shrugged. "He's got his own fight now. Uncle Jac's sick. You asked why I am here... well, Mum wanted me to come and keep an eye on him... help him out some. We've done it under the guise that

I've gone as far as I could with the smithy I was with, and I need to learn from someone with his level of expertise. Which is true. Sort of. Two birds, one stone. Mum is reassured he has family around... and I'm back in Uncle Jac's workshop, getting experience under a true master at the same time."

"I didn't realise he was not well, but I'm glad he's got family here with him. So, you're just here until he gets better?"

"He reckons I'm here to learn, but Rachel... I don't think Uncle Jac is going to get better any time soon. He's slowing down. It shocked me when I arrived. It is worse than I expected. I'm no medical man, but this is like watching a candle burn out. He hides it pretty well, but he's not in a good way."

"Oh, Cob. I'm so sorry!"

"I'm sorry too, but we came here to clear your head, not air my problems and cloud up the atmosphere even more."

"Perhaps it is what we both need. I've realised that if I can have just two hours to myself in the morning, it seems like I can pretty much manage everything else all day. When I have that time... it feels like the ride coming out here: just the rhythm of the horse's hooves pounding. It's so nourishing, alive, energising! But if I don't get that time in the workshop, I feel like I'm drowning in monotony and routine. Smithy's workshop has been my lifeline, but now, suddenly it is being pulled away from me. Every morning something or someone encroaches on my time and interrupts me. It seems I am not allowed to have just two hours to myself!"

Cob looked up at the moon and saw the silhouettes of bats winging past. He could hear the ripples of the creek water running in the gully close by, unseen in the night shadows. "What if you had your own studio? Like Uncle Jac said… your own space. Then you wouldn't have to share. You're less likely to be interrupted if not right there in the Homestead compound. If it's harder for others to access, you would get your uninterrupted couple of hours."

"What a dream that would be! Are you suggesting this shed could be my studio?"

"It's not being used. It is private… cute little creek setting. Has a very rustic art-studio feel."

"This? But… there is no forge. I need a forge."

"It would be simple enough to set the whole place up. Your forge wouldn't need to be big. Not like you are shipbuilding," he said with a grin.

"Oh, I think my shipbuilding could be accommodated here easily. Oh, this is a wonderful idea! Yes, this would be perfect. Perfect in every way."

"Well… if you can convince your father, I'd happily help you fix the place up. And I am thinking it might me a good idea to keep the meddling Lincroft out of it for as long as you can. Maybe hint it is something benign and boring… like an oil-painting studio… or basket weaving."

"Really? Basket weaving? You have no more faith in my craft than the next person!"

"Hey. I'm just suggesting you peddle it in a way that keeps them from interfering. If they think oil painting is a more lady-like pursuit than anvils and metal forging… it might mean they are less obstructive. Up to you how you handle it. I've seen you with your father. I reckon you'll work it out."

"I guess..." she conceded. Perhaps he was right. Oil painting it would be.

"Cob?"

"Yes, Mr Leybourne?" He put down the horses' hoof he was working on and stood up. He loosened the neck scarf from under his collar and ran it up over his forehead, wiping his brow.

"Rachel has an idea that she wants to set up the old Shepherd's hut as an art studio. Go out there with her and see if you can't talk her out of it."

Why would he try and talk her out of it? He suggested it. He nodded soberly. "Yes, Sir."

"And if you can't, make sure it is safe and she has everything she needs to make it work for her. It used to be a decent sort of hay shed, but it is so out of the way we don't use it unless all the other sheds are full. It would need some clearing out. I can't imagine it has any of the potential she suggests. I've ordered a couple of windows from town just in case. Just humour her. She seems a bit down in the dumps lately, so a diversion like this might brighten her up."

"How much time do you want me to spend on it for you, Sir? If she decides she wants to go ahead that is..."

"Well, work on it in the mornings but have her back here before lunch. Oh. And don't broadcast it. She specifically asked that the project be kept private so that it functions as an artist's retreat for her. Oil canvases are the next thing apparently. Better than anvils that's for sure."

"Yes, Mr Leybourne," Cob said soberly. And he smiled broadly has he turned back to the horse he was shoeing and picked up its hoof.

6.

Smithy Jac made Rachel a solid metal stand and rack; her own portable forge custom made to her height. They had scrounged around and found an array of bricks to line it. Rachel sorted through the accumulated tools in the workshop, and they loaded the cart with an anvil, portable bellows... and an assortment of tools and tongs that weren't being used. Cob added bags of coal to the load, and Rachel put in a covered breakfast hamper before she climbed up beside Cob. "Where are the windows that Father said you were to install?"

"They haven't arrived yet. But we can set up the forge and workshop first," he said, as he flicked the reigns and the horse pulled forward in the harness. They headed out the gate towards the hut. "And then I thought that, if you wanted to start working on having your daily artistic respite, I can keep sorting out the rest of it. You won't be restricted to two hours while I am at your service, because I have been instructed to stay to help you until this studio is arranged to your satisfaction. Just so long as you are back by lunch."

"Really? You mean this is entirely authorised, and we don't have to go sneaking around?" She grinned delightedly and stretched her arms to the sky. "That seems utterly too much good fortune."

"My involvement depends on how elaborate you intend your rustic artist studio will be." He put it out there like a tester. What would she choose?

She laughed. "You know, I feel that this studio is going to be a very demanding project with many difficult problems that you will need to solve every morning. It could require a lot of work, which

43

means I should be able to progress with my sculpture much faster than I thought!"

Ahh, yes. The sculpture. Of course. Cob pulled on the reigns to steady the horse as the cart lurched over a rut in the track. Uncle Jac's wisdom echoed around in his head as a severe caution: *a guaranteed dead end for sure.*

They took out the crosscut saw and found a large fallen tree, and together they cut a substantial block from its trunk to mount the anvil. They used the harness horse to pull it into place at the centre of her workshop. Cob set up the forge and Rachel put it to work, making shelf brackets, and other workshop racks for her tools. Together they constructed a solid workbench and mounted her vice. She brought in an unused kitchen hutch from one of the workers' cottages, to hold her notebooks and design journals. She even set up her easel with her artist paints, brushes, and canvases as well. Over the course of weeks, it was emerging as Rachel's creative haven. It was a wonderful moment when she swung a forged metal sign: "The Shepherd's Studio", over the front door. It swung on a shepherd's crook, and she even added the figures of a shepherd holding a lamb... which looked surprisingly like Jesus.

Every morning, when they drove the cart out there, it was like crossing international borders into a peaceful armistice zone away from all the politics of the homestead. There was no one to whinge about bent hatpins; or the unfair deal of their hand of cards; or the stodgy density of their cake. Here, it was a place of energetic discussion, light laughter, quiet industry, and grateful appreciation. To Rachel, it was how she imagined church should be... a place of worship. A place of gratitude. A place of replenishing, communion, and companionship.

Finally, the day arrived when Jac enlisted some workmen to help manoeuvre the support frame holding Rachel's sculpture on to the back of the cart. Cob strapped it down tight, and Rachel hovered over its transport all the way out to the Shepherd's hut. They stopped a couple of times to tightly secure the tie-downs. "How are we going to get the frame off the cart?"

He shrugged unperturbed. "I've brought planks to make up a ramp. It will be slow, but we can ease it down using ropes and a winch. Once it is in place, you can get back to it, and the bonus of a dedicated space is that you won't have to keep packing it away."

"Ahh, yes. That is what I need to do. Dedicate the studio." Rachel went and picked up her bible. She pulled some linseed oil from her painting case and walked to the centre of the studio. Cob removed his hat as she poured it onto the ground. Rachel turned to Psalm 84.

"How amiable are thy tabernacles, O LORD of hosts!
My soul longeth, yea, my heart and my flesh crieth out for the
living God. Yea, the sparrow hath found an house,
and the swallow a nest for herself...
Blessed are they that dwell in thy house..."

Cob affirmed that with a definite "Amen."

"Now, I am ready! It's been ages. I just want to feel the ring of steel on the anvil again."

Cob smiled. Evidently all the other smithing jobs she had been doing to set the studio up didn't count. She inspected the minor damage to the structure of her sculpture that was incurred during transport and fired up the forge. It was a great sensation to feel that rhythm pounding through her body as she worked. Very soon the repairs were made, and she was completely immersed in adding to the next section of the hull.

Part of the routine they developed was eating breakfast from Billie's basket hamper, cooking farm fresh eggs on a metal plate placed over the forge-fire and making billy-tea. This morning, as they sat with the rising sun streaming through the door, there was a smear of char on Rachel's cheek. It felt comfortable, being here together, sitting on low stumps, eating without interruption, listening to the magpies and currawongs along the creek warbling their morning choir-song.

"I like being here... having breakfast and a morning cup of tea in a rough mug," Rachel said with a smile. "I enjoy this more than our breakfast parlour even with the fine china, that's for sure." She rotated a large campfire fork over the coals so that the slab of bread threaded on it browned evenly. The rich warm smell of toast filled the shed. She slathered it with freshly churned butter and lashings of wild rosella jam.

"And here I was thinking you didn't like breakfast at all. I have seen you turn down company on numerous occasions, even preferring starvation to having someone encroach on your forge-and-anvil time."

She scoffed. "I like breakfast and I only turn it down because I want more time to work. Here I have plenty of time."

"My mother would say that breakfast is the most important meal of the day. I've noticed you have not always shown that kind of devotion to it."

"Huh. I know who you are referring to, and I would happily go for forty days and forty nights without eating breakfast at all, if it meant I could avoid a morning with *him*."

"Really? I thought you liked Mr Lincroft."

"Where on earth would you get that idea?"

"I recall a whole series of anxious scenarios that occur whenever Lincroft showed up at the workshop. It even involved the ultimate compliment – suggesting I am the creator of your sculpture. This project is quite beyond my capabilities by the way, so I trust that I am never challenged to prove my contribution, or you will be exposed."

"I get immersed in it and he catches me off guard. It doesn't mean anything."

He grinned. "You hurriedly jump into a skirt; you arrange your hair just so; you pretend you don't know how to hold a hammer. It is an instinctive, deceitful little twist to your regular mornings. So, I guess I assumed you would only go to all that trouble if you liked him. And I confess I also assumed that you wanted to make a good impression on a man who otherwise might not approve of coal fires and forges."

"Huh! What I actually thought was that he would betray me if he saw the truth of what I was doing there. My family likes him. I don't share their enthusiasm."

"You don't? Why?"

"I'm not giving an inventory of his failings. It would mean we would be talking about him way too long. I would much rather focus on something more interesting... like, how are we going to transport my sculpture when it is not just a hollow frame, but fully complete?"

He raised his brow at her evasion on the subject of Walter Lincroft. With a slight turn of his head, he looked past her to the sculpture. Sections were gradually filling in like a canvas being blocked in with coloured paint. "Well, moving it out here worked pretty well, and it has given us a good idea of how it transports. I think we could reasonably expect to do the process in reverse. I was thinking about using the scaffolding you have, as the framework to build a solid platform under it that will function as a sled. The extra weight will mean we'll need a full team of horses, and I'll enlist some help to glide it along, particularly across the gullies, as there are a couple of sections where the track isn't great. But when you're ready, I'm confident the installation at the front entrance should be a smooth enough process."

She stared at him with a frown.

"Did I say something wrong? I'm pretty sure that will work."

"Quite the contrary. Cob, do you realise you are the only person, aside from Smithy Jac, who takes me seriously? ... you really believe this will be finished and installed."

He shrugged and grinned. "Perhaps it's a family trait... blind loyalty to the trade; gullible confidence in a fellow smith."

"You say that like we are equals, and you are totally convinced in this project being completed. It seems you know with absolute certainty that one day it will be out there, standing as a beacon of welcome to everyone who comes to Shipman Downs, just like I have dreamed. My father assumes I will never finish it... or shouldn't."

"That's faith, isn't it? Just knowing, that you know what you know, without having to justify it. I honestly don't see too many people this committed to any sort of project, much less an artistic one. Of course, its destiny will be realised. You have invested too much already."

"Thank you, Cob. Your faith in this, is a remarkable gift. I appreciate it."

He nodded. "You're welcome, Miss Leybourne. You will make sure it gets to reside where it belongs. I know it." And he went back to work on the casement framework for fitting the windows. As Cob sawed and hammered, he wondered about another idea of belonging; a parallel destiny was firmly encasing his heart. Perhaps his confidence in that matter was less certain, but it definitely qualified as blind and gullible.

"I cannot come out here tomorrow, Cob. Aunt Dorothea and my cousins are finally leaving. I am required to accompany them to town, along with everyone else, to say farewell."

He titled his head and brushed his hair out of his eyes. "It seems you survived after all. Perhaps, in the end, their visit was not the ordeal you supposed it was going to be."

"It's not over yet. I still have to get through tomorrow."

"Just one more day. Even though their visit lasted longer than you expected, it seems you have endured it well enough."

"The only thing that has made it manageable has been this: my Shepherd's Studio. My mornings with you. Being here, working on my sculpture... that is what has kept me sane. Outside of this... I have no idea how I would have managed it."

"Glad to be of service. Tell me, you said your relatives come every year. Why was it worse this time? I thought by now you would have some sort of routine... like Christmas, the types of things we do as family, that we don't always enjoy."

"Because every year it gets worse. From the moment they turn up, they spend their time demeaning my home, my clothes, my pastimes, my horse, and my boots. They despise that I love this life and the isolation here. Every detail associated with it is constantly compared to how it does not measure up to what they have in town. How many times have they told me how much they miss civilisation? If they love it so much, they should just stay there!"

"Your sister seems to welcome their company. Are you so different?"

"Like chalk and cheese! It is a marvel how two sisters could be so different. Leah hates it here almost as much as Aunt Dorothea, so they share it as a common bond of solidarity. I thought for sure, she would offer to take Leah back to town with her to visit this time. Leah certainly has hinted often enough... but Aunt Dorothea seems totally deaf to her suggestions."

"Why wouldn't they take her when she wants it so much?"

"I think it is because they know Leah is already a convert and she doesn't need convincing of the benefits of town. I, on the other hand, need the advantage of their enlightenment. And... this is embarrassing... they have it in their heads that Leah is not pretty enough. It is insulting and rude, but they are oblivious to how hurtful such ignorance is. Since they consider me the handsomer sister, they think that I should have the privilege of their preening society. Aunt Dorothea has already asked me to go back with them a number of times. But I won't go." She stared at him, almost as if she was daring him to challenge her resolve.

But all he did was shrug. "Seems to me that you are one who will not have your mind made up for you. If you wanted to explore the upper echelons of society, then I imagine it would not be too hard for you to extract such an invitation. I also think that your determination to stay closer to your own stamping ground is equally within your means."

Rachel looked at him curiously. "You are not the usual sort of blacksmith, Cob Horne. I don't understand you."

"Not sure what there is to understand. I can work a forge. My uncle is dying. I am hoping... when the time comes, to be promoted to his role in the workshop if I can demonstrate my competence at the skills, in spite of my apparent inexperience and age."

"Hmm. You seem as skilled as any. But..."

"But...?"

"I don't know. It's just odd. I don't know any other blacksmith who would identify the *'upper echelons of society'* as even a thing. Where did you learn to talk like that?"

He grinned at her. And shrugged again. "Oh, I don't know..." he said evasively.

"Come on... of course you know. You are different. Tell me."

"Okay. I may have been influenced, a little, during my intern placement as a legal clerk, under my godfather's recommendation." He grinned at the shock on her face. "The legal profession is quite particular about phrasing and the choice of words, whether you work out the back sorting through files, or dealing with people coming in for legal counsel. You are very astute Miss Rachel to notice that... and I was sloppy not to be swearing like a ringer to throw you off the scent." The other part... about his strict English masters at private school and growing up with varied and vigorous conversations around dining tables and drawing rooms... that didn't need mentioning... not yet.

"Why would you hide such an education? That can't be a bad thing."

"Why would you hide your passion for sculpture? That can't be a bad thing either."

"Yes, but when people expect something in particular, they are not so generous about it being different to what they predict."

"Exactly! I could not agree more."

"So, what happened? A clerk's pen is a long way from a blacksmith's hammer."

"Huh. I happened, I guess. Didn't really like it. The idea was that my Uncle Ruben wanted me to try it out, to see if I would be interested in pursuing a legal career. If I had, he would have sponsored me through university. I just couldn't see it. It's not me. I prefer this. I have good memories of spending time with Uncle Jac when I was little. I was the regular little convert from an early age. You know the axiom: *Teach a kid, when they are young, the way they should go and when they are old, they will not depart from it.* That's me. This got stuck in my bones, and I came back to it. I am happiest here."

"Oh my! I think that is the best way to actually describe what I feel. That is it exactly! When I am here... I feel at home, and I am happiest."

"Well, Miss Rachel, it has been my honour to be the means of effecting your happy escape."

She smiled and thought it was ironic that Walter had declared that he had wanted the privilege of being the tool of her escape. His version felt like prison. This was better, freer, and more satisfying, by far!

⁕

7

They piled out of the buggies, that were lined up along the street in a cavalcade. This annual farewell ritual was given as much consequence as every other aspect of their country vacation: the tea, the lunch, the coffee, the strolling through the community garden, the lingering hugs, and the emotional well-wishes on the train platform. Rachel swallowed and sighed as she stepped down from the buggy, pulling her green leprechaun gown and her matching grouchy goblin attitude into submission. Leah was already wiping her fogging eyeglasses in a demonstrative show of her disappointment that their visit was over.

Rachel turned away. She wondered how it would be received if she could be as transparently honest about her feelings. She was pretty sure her expressions would sound like a New Year's Eve party: banging on pots and pans; blowing homemade paper party trumpets; waving her kerchief; cheering and clapping as their train rolled out of town. Rachel closed her eyes and groaned, then straightened up and gave a wan little smile as Aunt Dorothea came to her side. "I know, Rachel my dear. I know how upsetting this is. However, there is still time for you to change your mind if you would like to come with us for a little respite from country life."

"Hmm. Unfortunately, I have not packed a travel-case."

"Oh, pish, Rachel my dear. We could sort something, I am sure."

"Again, Aunt Dorothea, I am grateful for the opportunity... but not this time." *Or any time!* Internally she was stamping her foot for emphasis.

Rather than complaining or trying to change her mind, Aunt Dorothea patted her shoulder and nodded knowingly. Rachel looked at her warily. "Perhaps this is for the best, Rachel my dear. Perhaps this is for the best..." And she shuffled the waiters around to arrange the tables for their lunch at the café. Rachel suspiciously considered Aunt Dorothea's willingness to raise a white flag and retreat. But as Rachel watched her aunt frown and smile, and organise, and reorganise the seating for their luncheon to her satisfaction, she rebuked her own apprehension and acknowledged that her aunt just had bigger battles to wage this morning. The effort required to exit with pizzazz was obviously taxing.

Finally, they were escorted to their table. Walter lingered by Rachel's side and pulled out her chair. Then he manoeuvred his own close beside her. He was amusing and attentive while their drinks were brought out. His smile was congenial as they served their food. Rachel noticed Leah frown when Cousin Felix tried to match Walter's antidotes. His attempts at being droll just ended up sounding more pompous than usual. Walter ordered the wine and declared a dramatic toast in tribute to closing an affable season at Shipman Downs. He pledged to continue to enjoy its pastural pleasures in their stead until the completion of his designated term. Then he would resume life in civilisation and promised to meet up with them for many a sociable occasion.

Finally, everyone rose to go for a stroll in the community park, to observe the pleasantness of the gardens before their train departed. Rachel frowned as Walter accosted one of the waiters and berated him about some unsatisfactory aspect of his service. Rachel reluctantly went to follow her cousins, but Aunt Dorothea placed a restraining hand on her forearm. Rachel was stuck, and for the first time since they had arrived, she now earnestly desired she *could* join her cousins so she would not be detained. Aunt Dorothea leant over and spoke in a hushed voice. "Rachel my dear... such excellent news! I have been wanting to tell you since I was made aware. I was asked not to say, but we are shortly leaving, so what can be the trouble now? Walter has been given his third obligation. We knew it was coming, and now we are in a fever of anticipation because we finally know what it is!"

Rachel looked around and noticed the red face of the waiter who was now also being harassed by his supervisor. Rachel tried to quickly think of a way to extract herself from this little interview. "This sounds entirely exciting for you, Aunt," she said.

"Oh, not as much as it is for you, Rachel my dear. Walter has been commissioned to find a wife! How about that? A wife!"

"A wife? He seems to enjoy his single life satisfactorily. What would he do with a wife?"

"Exactly, Rachel my dear. Exactly. Choosing a wife will establish evidence of his maturity and how he is able to demonstrate the stability and sobriety fitting of his inheritance. As soon as it was determined from the correspondence from his uncle, that this is his next obligation, Walter has indicated that he will comply with this requirement before his season at Shipman Downs is finalised. He is going to marry! And Rachel my dear, I must say, this is looking very promising for you."

"Promising? Whatever do you mean, Aunt Dorothea?" she said, her face flushing bright red, matching the humiliation of the waiter by the door. Oh, how she hoped it was not what she thought was being suggested!

"I would not like to speak out of turn, or make your hopes soar prematurely, but it would be completely appropriate for Walter to consider *you* for the role." She spoke very rapidly, her excitement almost getting the better of her.

"He would consider *me* to be his wife? You must be kidding!"

"I know, Rachel my dear. I know. It seems an impossible turn of good fortune! But I am convinced, given how attentive he has been in general, and particularly how he was at lunch, that it is a *very* strong possibility that you are the favoured contender. Oh, how wonderful this is! And all of this, is entirely because of my obliging advocation on your behalf. This is *so* perfect in every regard! Now you must stop scowling and put on a congenial smile and catch up to your cousins to enjoy a stroll about the gardens."

8.

Rachel was quiet and sullen all the way out to the studio. Cob tried a couple of times to engage her, but she refused to be drawn into any sort of conversation, so in the end he left her to brood. Even before the cart had pulled to a stop outside the studio, Rachel jumped down and quickly opened up the doors, within moments she had fired up the forge, and she was banging and clanging and thumping the iron into submission in a furious whirl of pent-up energy.

Cob let her go, but eventually he handed her a mug of coffee and indicated that he had laid out breakfast from the basket. "Do you want to tell me what's the matter?" he asked.

She took the drink and gulped. But rather than sitting on one of the low stumps, as they normally did, she paced around the shed. "You want to know what this is about?" she threw at him.

"Yeah. Have I done something? I don't know what's going on," he said.

"I will tell you exactly what is going on! They are all plotting their next move. Or, more accurately, *my* next move! We have finally found out what Walter's mysterious third duty is. He is tasked with finding a wife. A wife! And it seems he has targeted *me* to fulfill that duty! They are fixing the race so I have to marry Walter Lincroft before he leaves Shipman Downs. That is precisely what everyone wants and from all indications, it is exactly what Walter expects as well." She stared at him, her face blanching in terror.

Cob was still for a while, his heart beating at a wild pace. Relief that he had not offended her in some unintentional way, was displaced by the look of dread in her eyes. He felt it wash over him so that the news became his own horror almost in the same instant. "So, you don't want to... you know... marry him?"

"Of course I don't! How could you think I would even consider marrying that pompous, self-important, indulged, arrogant, spoilt...?" Words failed to form. Her eyes fired hot like the forge coals she had used all morning.

"Okay. That's something. Not keen." That was one thing at least.

"Not *keen*! I hardly think that is strong enough. He doesn't even like me! He doesn't like what I like. He doesn't like that *I like* what I like! He doesn't respect me. He doesn't allow me to hold any opinions that aren't aligned with his perfectly set out world. Why would I marry him? He's a miserable parasite!"

"Heard he was rich. Wouldn't that make you the parasite?"

"Huh! Allowing that creature to latch himself to me would kill me like poison, sucking my life away. Or perhaps it would not be as slow. This is more aligned to an execution!"

"He could offer you a comfortable life..." This was something, that as a blacksmith, he didn't hold in his hand to offer. Not to that level.

"But you forget: he is not even wealthy yet. At the moment he's running on credit of what could be. All he offers is a life of what *might be*... one day. More than comfortable probably... if I help him tick off the criteria set down by his uncle. There is so much riding on this, for Father and Mother as well. I know I am not going to have a say. I have no way of escaping this. Oh Cob! What am I going to do?" Tears of fear spilt over her lashes as she continued to pace.

Cob looked at her silently, and prayed for a way in... "What if someone else married him? If he only needs to tick the box it shouldn't matter who does it."

"He won't though. I believe he has already told my parents that he wants to marry *me*. The fact that Father owns property – it has an appropriate feel of landed gentry; wool to support the textile industry in which his uncle is a very influential importer and exporter. Walter seems to have completely forgotten that when he came here, he despised our poor country simplicity. The man is a fraud!"

"And what about you? Is there someone you would marry?"

"Oh, Cob – if only you would! You understand how I think. You never dismiss me. You listen to me. You respect me. You encourage me in every regard."

"We've barely known each other two months."

"I met Walter the same day I met you. If I have to marry on a short acquaintance, I prefer you. Hands down."

He had to say it. "Short or otherwise, I know I hold something that he doesn't... I love you, Rachel." He tracked her pacing around the studio.

Rachel gasped and continued on without a pause. "Well, that is not helping! How is this declaration helping me? How hard is it to know, that on one hand I am loved and respected? Yet the man I am destined for, is everything that you are not?"

He looked at her and said nothing for a long while. Eventually she calmed her pacing and looked at him. "I love you," he repeated as he reached out and held her hands. Heartfelt.

"Oh, Cob. Marry me!"

"You would ask me to marry you? Rachel... I... you know how this would look? I am a blacksmith."

"I don't care. We can elope. We can go away, and I'll never have to look at his face again."

"I am not going to elope."

"So, you do not love me after all? Would you lie about this? If you truly did, you would do this!"

"Rachel. I would not lie to you. I *do* love you. But this is the very reason that I will not subject you or your family to the shame of an elopement. The disgrace would mean we would have to leave Shipman Downs and never come back. This whole thing is not acceptable to you in the first place because of the expectation of you leaving."

"Cob, if I have to leave anyway, I would leave with you. Not him! Please!"

"We get married in a church, before God and witnesses, ... or not at all. It is the way it should be."

Rachel stared at him and saw the resolve in the set of his shoulders and the gaze of his eye. She burst into tears. "You have just condemned me to death!" she cried.

Cob stood up and swore, turning away. "What a mess!"

Her hot anger did not abate. She stared at him through her tears. "Agreed! And what is more... Walter Lincroft does not care! To him it is not messy. It is just a game... a game of cards... or dice. He is only invested in this so completely, because to him there is the challenge of winning. He made a declaration when he first arrived that he would change my mind on him. He thinks I have thrown down the gauntlet... and dared him to prove himself in this matter. He is convinced he has to prevail regardless of the cost. And when he wins, once again his arrogance is validated. Everyone around him loses one way or another... but it is like they are completely blinded by his social credentials and do not see the game he plays.”

Cob heard her. He closed his eyes. He could hear the creek running over the rocks, hurrying away to escape. He opened his eyes and turned slowly around to face her. “Say that again...”

“To him it is a game of cards... or dice. He is only invested in the challenge of winning. Everyone around him does not see the game he plays.”

“Not everyone. We do.”

She shrugged. “So? He still thinks it is his God-given right to prevail; that he has a blessed inherited predisposition to success; and that his talented tendency is only to be dealt excellent good luck. What is most horrifying, is that he might actually be right!”

“But if it is a game... then surely that offers us a different set of rules.”

“I don’t understand...”

“If this was about the morality of rich-versus-poor, or good-versus-bad... or kind-versus-cruel... then those rules are fairly well understood and established. But you said this is the game of winning and losing to him. That has a different set of rules all together.”

“I still don’t understand...”

“So... everyone sitting at a card table has equal opportunity to win the game by the way they play their hand. Lincroft has been playing the game on the assumption that no one is on to him. Or if they are, they would never be bold enough to challenge his hand or call his bluff. It’s a pretty poor game that offers no competition, or if one expects to win without any contest or battle of wits.”

Rachel turned back and locked eyes with Cob, tracking his logic with a tilt of her head. Something like hope was burning holes in her head, and she stared unblinking into his face as he continued. "Lincroft's smugness is his flaw... his tell... his weak hand. But what if... what if we pick up the glove and accept this challenge? What if we run with it, and find out who is actually going to win this contest of wits? But if we did that, we would not be able to give even the slightest hint that anything is different to what he believes. You must understand this Rachel: if we choose to engage in this game of his... the stakes are high: very high. Winning will be our life... and losing will be death."

⁂

9.

"I hardly can believe your vanity, Rachel. No one is good enough for you. Why can you not see that Walter is amiable, respectable, dependable, and not to mention financially stable."

"There are a lot of '*ables*' in his qualifications. What about 'insufferable, horrible, and unbearable'? It sounds like you would really be open to marrying him yourself."

"Of course I would! But it seems that, once more, you despise an opportunity that I would be grateful for. Yes, once more, I am passed over and Rachel holds all the cards."

Rachel almost smiled. There was that metaphor of the card-table again. It was like a sign for her. "Leah, why do you suppose that my life is so favoured, and you are the object of everyone's disdain. Surely you can see that I would gladly swap places."

"You say that to try and soothe my disgust. But I am sorry, Rachel, I am not sure I can feel so amiable towards you in this. I am your older sister... and I don't even have anyone willing to look in my direction. Yet you have people trying to tackle you for the privilege of marriage. Once again Rachel wins."

"Leah, when did our lives become a competition? I would dearly love to see you happy. But marrying someone like Walter Lincroft? Is that really the way to achieve it? He is impossible to love."

"Love? Why do you assume that marriage has to be about love? Your romantic notions, Rachel, are as impractical as the iron sculptures that clutter our garden. There are other realistic considerations that are entirely far more likely to endure."

"Really, Leah! I cannot believe that you do not consider love enduring! It is one of the Big Three: faith, hope, and love. These three remain. These are the enduring virtues that God had given us. The greatest of these is love. You know that!"

"I know that marriage can function without romance. I see it all the time. It is only you who holds to the idea that love has to be the prerequisite to a functioning relationship. It might the last of your vain, useless, artistic, idealistic notions that you will have to set aside. It is time to grow up."

"How can you even say that? I could never willingly marry without love... even if it is that practical, sensible sort of love that respects and regards kindly. It is impossible to consider it otherwise."

"Well, you will find out soon enough. Mother is determined that Walter Lincroft does not leave Shipman Downs without a ring on her daughter's hand."

"Ahh yes... but which daughter...?" Rachel left the question dangling. Tantalising. Silence.

"What are you suggesting, Rachel?"

She shrugged. "I have realised something. You accuse me of always getting my way... of being the family favourite... the spoilt one... the one that everyone panders to. I admit I never really gave much credence to this, because you are constantly cast up before me as the glowing example to follow. But I do wonder, how many times have you stepped aside to allow me my way? I am sorry, Leah. I truly am. I haven't been considerate of what *you* want."

"Oh, Rachel, I don't want to sound bitter and perverse... but you are so gloriously blessed, and you don't even realise it! Father dotes on you; and Mother corrects my posture. It has been that way forever."

"So, what is it you want, Leah? Really, if you could have anything... what would that be?"

"I want to leave Shipman Downs. I do! There I have said it! I envy you so much, that you are satisfied here. But this place is dry and confined... even in the good seasons. It lacks culture, and society, and the relief of community diversions. The only way I can leave, is to marry. But it seems the only marriages available to me will merely move me further down the valley... and that is not far enough. Not far enough away at all!"

"Huh. It seems your purpose in a husband, is to be your ticket out of here."

"I know you despise my lack of contentment... but I have never fitted well here. And you have." She shook her head desolately. How could two sisters be so polarised in what they want? "Rachel, I know you don't get it. And I wish it was different... but it is not."

"Leah, it is my observation that I potentially could have a fiancé who would meet all your requirements in a spouse."

Leah stared at her sister wide-eyed in the lamplight, her eyeglasses making her eyes seem even larger than usual. "You are tormenting me with this idea. Don't mock me, Rachel. That is more humiliating than anything you have managed so far. Don't do it!" And she left the room in a rush, slamming the door behind her.

At dinner Rachel smiled and laughed and reeled Walter in closer by attentively listening to his wonderful stories of amusement. He relaxed into her smile and the wine he was drinking. Mother nodded and was more satisfied with everything. Leah glowered in disgust behind her eyeglasses at the charming little duo they were making over dessert. Afterwards they played cards, and Rachel surrendered to his competence, and he consoled her with some good instruction on how to improve her strategy and offered to play another hand as an opportunity for him to demonstrate his expertise... all for her improvement and edification of course.

Afterwards, when Leah came into their room, Rachel was at the washstand scrubbing her neck. "Ugh! The man is filth! I feel so contaminated. I don't know how you do it!"

"You surely looked like you were enjoying yourself well enough. You are a fake, Rachel Leybourne. A fraud to the core!"

"I know it. But if this is going to work, Leah... Walter must never know. He must never know I despise every pore of his despicable body. I despise his unblinking, emotionless eyes, and his charming, nauseating tales, and his self-absorbed, self-promoting parading. A peacock in full plumage is more humble! I just want to pluck, stuff, and bake him... and then feed him to the pigs!"

"Rachel! You have to settle down! Lower your voice. They are going to hear."

"I don't care, Leah. I don't care! I am not kidding here. This is something I am *never* going to come to terms with, or eventually be reconciled to. You have to know that! I feel like am on the brink of going stark raving crazy!"

"Why don't you just tell him? Or at least you could tell Father. He is always on your side."

"Except in this situation, Leah, you are the only one who sees my dilemma. You, my dear sister, are the only sensible and sane one left in this house. I have told Walter that you are the better bride, but it is beyond his comprehension and vanity to consider that he is incapable of wooing me around. He assumes that his resolve to convert all my incompetencies will quickly transform me into the lady of culture he imagines I should be. My hope is that if I let the charade persist, and he believes he is winning his campaign for my improvement, he will eventually be satisfied or bored, and drop his obnoxious attention. Father is relieved that Shipman Down's future is stabilised by the Lincroft promises of financial security. Mother is relieved that she has a daughter getting married. You and I are the only ones who see the truth."

"Well, I wish I could be as deluded. There would be some relief in the anaesthetic of ignorance."

"Or... you could consider what I offer with measured, clear-headed, deliberate, calculated vision. You deserve to have your chance too, Leah. You are smart and gracious and kind. I seriously don't think Walter deserves you, but if you are willing to go through with this, I would be more relieved than I can say."

Leah sat on the side of the bed. "Rachel, I actually suspect you are serious. How could you propose such a thing? We would be forever shamed!"

"Except for one thing. You have forgotten the vanity of the man we are dealing with. He will do whatever it takes to cover his pride and reputation. And in the end, he will make it all seem like his idea. This is my hope! My glorious hope! This is the golden thread that will tie it all together. This is the way for you to get your ticket out of the valley. And for me to marry someone I actually like. But we need to do it together. We need to have each other as allies in this to make it even plausible. Because, unfortunately, I cannot see our parents even remotely accommodating the audacity of this plan. So, this is on us... beginning to end. Are you up for that?"

10

"You said you did a sitting once, and I wanted to ask if you might like to humour me and do it again." She smiled a charming smile, winsome in its invitation.

Walter turned to Rachel and nodded. "I could be lured into accommodating your little pastimes, which have consumed so much of your attention. So, would this mean you'd show me your art-studio? I have heard it rumoured around that such a place exists."

"Oh, but of course it exists. However, I really must caution you, Walter. My studio is very stark. Nothing more than a barn. I have not shared this with you because I know it does not measure up to what is normally considered proper. To be honest, the studio is actually very primitive. Yet that means it is also private, and lonely, and lovely. I find it a wonderful place to be creative... all alone. I am a little embarrassed to ask, because perhaps I thought you would not like to see it. And I understand completely if you are reluctant, given how remote it is."

His eyes stirred with curiosity... and possibly lust. Improper and private? "So, you want me to support your newfound creativity by sitting for an oil portrait? I would very much like to see where you go almost every day."

Rachel nodded and smiled and thought he had no idea how far he was from really having a clue about anything. But this time he was the rat following her trail, deliberately set to lure him towards the cheese.

They rode out to the shed. As Rachel dismounted and tied Blaze under the trees. She frowned at the Blacksmith cart from the workshop, which was standing by the open door. "What's he doing here? Hello? Smithy? Is that you?" she called as she pushed the ajar door further open and went inside.

"Oh! Yes, Miss. But it is Cob. My uncle had me come and collect the rubbish, like you asked."

They walked further into the muted shadows of the barn. "Leah! What on earth are you doing here?" exclaimed Rachel.

"I asked Cob to bring me. You are always coming out here. I wanted to see what it is that has captivated your attention so."

"Well, you could have just asked me."

Walter looked annoyed. His plans for a private rendezvous into the lonely reaches of the station were thwarted by her sister's curiosity and the work-boy's duties. "Well, this is just *great*. I was going to do a sitting," he said, disdain mixing heavily with his irritation.

"No, no! This is perfect! We can still do it, because Leah has a very correct sense of light and colour. She is much more accomplished at oils than I am... so she can guide the sitting. And rather than do something that is all neat and sterile, the blacksmith boy has given me a grand idea. Cob can be your stand in."

Cob turned around and stared at her. "Sorry what?"

"You. I need you to be the stand in. I am going to paint a blacksmith scene. You can stand in for the main part. I can't expect Walter to have coal dust and stuff all over him... but then just for the last segment, I will complete the composition using Walter's face... because his face, and the set of his chin, is so very handsome." She swallowed and turned away, and hoped she sounded completely embarrassed by her fascination with Walter's fashionable good looks.

Walter nodded, receiving her admiration. And then he paused, frowned, and cringed. "You are going to paint me as a blacksmith? That is not flattering! This wasn't part of the deal."

"Well, I wasn't sure how I wanted to do it, but I like this idea. What do you think Leah?"

Leah broke out of her entranced gaze that had been locked in on Cob. "Yes. Yes, I think this is a very good idea. It will create a raw sense of energy." She also swallowed.

Walter frowned and was now confused. He pulled over a cut-off barrel used as a stool and sat close to where Rachel had set up her easel. "This is not at all what I expected. Very tedious..."

"Just be patient. You will get to see what I do, just as we planned, and I will be able to sit with you as soon as I start. Let me just set this up. Now, Cob... bring this over here. Hold the hammer like you do. Stand there. Leah? What do you think?"

"I think he needs to take his shirt off." Leah swallowed and blushed.

"Miss?" Cob frowned.

"This is purely an artistic choice. Your classic musculature is exactly what is needed for this sort of piece."

"*I* think I need to get back to the workshop." Cob started to walk back to his cart.

"No. No. Please! Leah has a point. I need you to do this."

"I'm not paid to be your artistic amusement. I have work that needs to be done. That is what your father pays me for."

"I think it is idiotic! I have never done anything so degrading... and since *I* am the blacksmith, that is not an unfamiliar notion!"

Walter strode over. "Smithy! You will do what the ladies require of you."

Cob looked him in the eye, began to burr up... and then backed right down. "If you say so, Mister," he said meekly.

Walter smirked. "I do say so. Now get to it!"

Leah stepped up and adjusted her eyeglasses. "Please, just let me talk with him." Rachel shrugged and took Walter back to the easel and gave him a mug of water, talking vaguely about the balance of composition, and the cast of light from the window, and the layering of colour. Walter was truly bored, and she kept burbling away in a monotone.

Leah spoke earnestly with Cob. And then there were some quiet exchanges. Eventually Cob took off his shirt and pulled his braces up over his bare shoulders. She took some char and ash from the cold fire pit and smeared it on his chest. Cob leant in and whispered something. Leah giggled and put her head to the side, and added some to his face, working it around like a make-up artist. She even ruffled his hair.

Walter sat staring at them and then suddenly sat up straight. He swore. "Your sister has a crush on the smithy!" he whispered to Rachel.

"Oh no. That is impossible. My sister is very appropriate."

"Rachel. Look at them! It is like watching a mating dance. This was her idea, remember. She didn't come to check out your studio. She came to check out the man-help. My goodness! Who would have thought your very plain, your very *odd* sister, had so much..." He stared at her as if seeing something completely unexpected.

Rachel cleared her throat and barged in to break up their private flirty moment. Cob was relaxed and smiled at Leah, and she smiled back... with another blush and a giggle. "Okay. So do you think this is going to work?" said Rachel in a very business-like tone.

"Oh yes," said Leah beaming. "I think it is working just fine." And she tilted her head less than subtly, adjusted her glasses, and gave Cob a full top-to-bottom inspection. "Just fine."

Rachel cleared her throat again, her face flushing hot, and she stood back to orchestrate the positioning of the model. The stance of his body over the anvil, the lift of the hammer, the twist of his torso. Rachel went back to the canvas and made some very deft strokes on the canvas. "No, no. The light is not right. Leah – hold this mirror and reflect the light onto the anvil and what he is crafting. That has to be the focal point. Straight. To the left. Come in closer. Yes, that is better. Hold that. Let me know when you need a break."

Leah sat, her back towards the easel where Walter sat, shining the reflected light from the mirror on Cob... breathing slowly to regulate her feelings. *Oh dear. How was this ever going to work?* One thing she did realise though: Rachel's infatuation with the smithy, was completely understandable. She no longer considered it demeaning, or beneath her sister to seek this alternate relationship. And it especially seemed reasonable when it paved the way for her own escape. "Keep your eye on the prize," Cob had whispered as she smeared coal dust on his chest. And she repeated that over and over to herself as a mantra, to settle her nerves, to still her trembling hand. *"Keep my eye on the prize."*

⁂

Rachel sat on her bed and braided her sister's hair. "Leah, what were you thinking, demanding Cob strip off like that? I seriously thought he was going to abandon the whole thing and leave. We need him. Don't forget he is an integral part of this plan."

She smiled mischievously. "I can't give you the head's up for every detail of our strategy and I am sorry if you felt unprepared. But some of it has to be spontaneous to be completely believable. I thought it was inspired! You worked with me, and it came off! If we are going to convince my family of this uncharacteristic move, I have to sell my involvement with Cob as something other than a fascination with his intellect. He is the blacksmith after all. So, I have to focus on something else and I also need a credible witness. Walter is that witness. And Cob was so charming about it. He said to me, *'Your boyfriend over there is quite intrigued with this little act.'* Walter was beside himself because he had enlisted Cob's services, just to have your attention fixated on his well sculptured body all morning. Cob was amused by the irony of that. And quite unexpectedly, I was enjoying myself immensely as well. Even more than an evening of card games I would say."

"Enjoy yourself by all means. Just don't go falling for him."

"Rachel. Are you jealous? Of me? Well, I am encouraged that I was so completely convincing. Just be reassured that I am concentrating on making this believable. And I am entirely focused on seeing this through. Right to the end." She paused and looked at her sister. "I get it, though. He is a good man," she said with a soft smile. "Cob has the heart of gentleman, even if he doesn't have the coat."

"Well, a coat is just wardrobe. My primary concern is how I am going to get through this without slogging Walter in the face. *And* did you notice I did my own version of play-acting when I called him handsome? How smug he looked! Augh! He's disgusting."

"Disgusting is in the eye of the beholder. I don't see him that way."

"How is it even possible that you think this way, my sensible Leah? Has your good sense *completely* gone by the way? However, I admit, I am beyond grateful just the same. You know, Leah, I like that we are working together as sisters on this. We haven't done that since... since that time I wanted to tackle mountain climbing."

"You mean when you were eight? And the mountain you chose to climb was the windmill? You had all the ropes, and the gloves, and the panicked rescuers complete with retrieval crew. Although, they were not playing with their imagination quite like you were. They were completely serious in their alarm."

Rachel smiled affectionately. "You're a good egg, Leah. A good egg."

"A good egg with spectacles. Sure."

"Of course. Those eyeglasses which you despise so intensely, are actually the defining element. They are exactly what we need to make you me... and me, you.

⁂

After dinner, Walter rearranged the table for his evening game of cards. Leah drew her mother aside and uncomfortably whispered, "I wonder if I could have an audience with Father and yourself, this evening... alone... now."

"Now? But Walter is setting up a game."

"Well, he can have his game, but I am your daughter, your *eldest* daughter, and I have requested a private audience with my parents. I don't ask for much, very often. I don't think this is unreasonable."

"Oh. Oh. Well, Walter could take Rachel for a walk perhaps."

"Yes. Good idea. A long walk."

"Oh? Leah. What is going on?" Her mother frowned.

"That is what I want to talk to you about."

Mr Leybourne sat uncomfortably on the lounge with his drink. His wife took her seat beside him with a severe purse to her lips. Leah sat down opposite them, slowly and soberly. "What is this about, Leah?" Mr Leybourne asked.

⁕

Walter opened the gate, and Rachel took his arm. She tried to disguise her tremor of revulsion as a shiver of delight, and she giggled and commented on how the evening was so very mild.

Walter sighed into the shadows. He was bored. This had not been as interesting as he had anticipated. It was so completely mundane. He had expected more resistance, more spunk, more excitement. In truth, he had thought more about Leah's little dance with the Smithy than his interactions with his own intended fiancé. This had turned tedious because of the need to go through the motions of social ritual. "You seem comfortable on my arm Rachel," he commented benignly.

She quickly pulled back her hand from his elbow. "Oh, I am sorry, Walter. It seems I have been presumptuous. I thought you liked having me on your arm."

"Well, yes. I do. It's just... well... that..."

"Well... what?" She stopped and turned to face him. "Have you changed your mind? Because if you have, now would be a good time to let me know."

He frowned. "What do you mean?"

"I mean that the very first evening you were here, you declared that you would change my mind about you. I remember thinking that would be impossible... but you challenged me to 'try you on' for size, like a fashionable hat. And so, I decided that was the least I could do. Yes, this is what I have done. I have been watching you carefully, Walter Lincroft. *Very* carefully ever since. You are charming, and witty, and my parents are quite taken with you and your fortune. I love my parents very much and their admiration is one of the greatest references a man can have."

"Oh. I thought you would be looking to... you know... fall in love."

"Really? Oh. I hadn't considered that. Do you think this is important?"

He took a deep breath. Had he been on the wrong track here? Unexpectedly that was a relief. "No, not at all. But I just thought that this might be something that you... well, most ladies, would consider a significant factor, if I were to ask her to marry me."

"If...?" and Rachel smiled into the dim moonlight and tittered charmingly.

"Well... I know that you are aware of my uncle's third obligation. He wants me to demonstrate my stability by choosing an appropriate wife."

"And... you think... well, do you still think that *I* could be your appropriate person?" Rachel couldn't bring herself to use the word '*wife*'. "Is this something that you see may last even beyond the need for distraction during your time here at Shipman Downs?"

"Of course."

"What makes me an appropriate choice, Walter? And don't say I have a pretty face, or I will hit you."

"Oh. Umm... Okay. Your father is a well-respected and well-regarded man of means... a landowner. Your mother has socially positioned relatives. You seem to be accomplished in matters of manners and society. And you like to read."

Rachel giggled again. "You surprise me, Walter. Very much. I thought you would be shallow, and superficial, and say that a pretty face was at the top of your list of your significant characteristics in potential bride."

"Oh... no. Not at all. I would choose you just the same, even if it was not the case. Although it can't hur..."

"Wow. So, there is substance in all of your considerations. I am impressed, Walter. You have actually given this a great deal of thought."

"Yes. Yes, I have. I would really like you to consider being my bride, Rachel. I love you."

"Oh, pfft Walter. You don't have to pretend. You know as well as I do, that we are not in love. But that is of no matter. You have already told me what aspects you value in an appropriate relationship, and these are more enduring that any fanciful romantic notions between us. I find it very reassuring, actually. So reassuring, in fact, that it seems that this is a proposal for marriage. Am I right, Walter? Do you want to marry a daughter of Shipman Downs?" And she gave him one of Aunt Dorothea's winning congenial smiles in the half-moon shining over the walkway where they strolled.

And he nodded. "I think I do. Yes. Will you marry me, Rachel?"

"I do think this moment deserves a bended knee. I have to be able to tell this tale with the appropriate number of amorous highlights."

He nodded and knelt in the dust. "Rachel Leybourne, will you do me the honour of being my bride? Will you marry me?" He pulled from his coat pocket a ring-box. He opened it and presented her with a very substantial ring.

She squealed and offered her left hand enthusiastically, her fingers extended. "Walter Lincroft, you are surpassing every expectation this evening. In every regard! This is absolutely in excellent taste. Oh! And look at the styling! It is so gloriously fashionable. This will certainly turn some eyes."

He nodded, reassured, as he stood up. And was grateful that the attendant in his uncle's office who dispatched the ring, had chosen one from an exclusive jewellery house noted for its elite craftsmanship. Rachel flashed it in the muted light, and hung dotingly on his arm, prattling meaningless affirmations, as they wandered around in the dark, taking the long route back to the homestead. She took a deep breath, relieved that he did not notice that she had not said "yes" in answer to his question.

⁂

Leah straightened her back against the lounge. "You asked what is this about? This is about me getting married. I want to get married." She stared at her parents through her spectacles, the pupils in her eyes looking ungainly and large.

"Leah. Have you lost your mind?" exclaimed her mother.

"Why is wanting to be married so ridiculous? I am of age. Well and truly."

"But this requires consideration and a suitable situation. It is not like ordering a new dress."

"Rachel is my junior by four years. It is proper that I should be married first. The shame is that there is a very real possibility of her getting married before me. This would be eternally hanging over my head. I *need* to be married first."

Her father shook her head bewildered. "And you want me to conjure up a groom for you, just like that. Sweetie, you know I would if I could..."

"Oh no. I have met someone. But I need you to consent. I need you not to be obstructive."

"Why would we be obstructive?" asked her mother bewildered. "If you have found someone..." It seemed to Leah, that her mother's confusion was based on the fact that it was beyond her comprehension she could have actually found anyone at all.

"Because he is the Smithy."

"Smithy Jac? Are you sure?"

"No! Of course not. He is ancient," she said in disgust. "No. No, his nephew: Theodore Jacob Ruben Horne. They call him Cob. Smithy Jac is his uncle."

"A tradesman? A smithy! Now you are truly out of your mind!"

Leah jumped to her feet. "Just about, Mother! I am out of my mind that Rachel has a suiter, and I could be left on the shelf and no one seems to even care! I am out of my mind that everyone notices her, and no one notices me. I am out of my mind that Cob is a very kind and generous person, and he would make a wonderful husband, as much as any gentleman, and yet he does not get a look in because he works to keep the machinery of our property going."

"Leah, sit down. This is very confusing. Do I need to call Wilhelmina for some smelling salts? You seem quite distraught."

"Oh, don't be patronising, Mother. I am quite well. I won't pretend to tell you that I am in love with him. But love is not the issue. Being married is."

"Are you sure?"

"Of course, I am sure. There is no way that Rachel is walking down an aisle with a groom on her arm, without me having done so first."

"But there were plans with Walter... to be married before he leaves."

"See! I knew it! He has already asked for her hand!"

"Well, yes, he has... but he doesn't seem inclined to extend his timeframes. We tried to negotiate that for Rachel. There isn't time for what you propose."

Leah's heart skipped a beat. Soon. So very soon. She sat down and recomposed herself and tried to sound reassuring. "I know. But it can be done. I have asked Cob to come and see you both. He is waiting outside on the verandah."

"Here? Now?"

"Yes, Mother. You have said so yourself, our timeframes are short."

"Well go and get him," said Mr Leybourne slowly.

Leah took a deep breath and went out to Cob who was sitting in the shadows. She nodded to him, and he stood up, holding a bunch of flowers in his hand. Before they went inside, he paused, his hand resting on her forearm gently. "Just so we are clear. I am asking for Rachel when we do this. Are you okay with that?"

She smiled. "Of course. I can't deny that I envy your feelings for each other, just a little bit. But when I see what you have, how can I not try and make a way for you both?" *And this is a way for me also,* she added in her mind. *For me, as well. Keep your eye on the prize...*

"Well, it is generous of you, Leah. We are grateful. Let's do this."

She opened the door, and in the light of the loungeroom, she could see Cob's rather old-fashioned, worn suit, crushed around the sleeves. He held the flowers awkwardly. Leah tried hard not to cringe. Yes, he did look very much like the smithy from the back shed, a fish out of water, floundering in the fashionable loungeroom of the homestead.

Mr Leybourne rose as he came in and shook Cob's hand. Mrs Leybourne nodded stiffly.

"So, Leah has given us an overview of the situation. It seems she would like to marry."

"Yes, Sir. I love your daughter very much." The rough skin on his knuckles was white as he gripped the stems of the cut flowers.

"Hmm. You think so?"

"Most sincerely, Sir. I am a hard worker, and an honest person. I think we can have a happy life together."

"And where are you going to live? You can't stay in the Smithy's shed loft."

"I have thought about this... and I was thinking about the Shepherd's hut. If the studio is no longer required after Mr Lincroft leaves with his wife... we could live there. I could make a suitable home for a daughter of Shipman Downs out there... away from the other workers... without making any statements of me trying to step above my station."

"Yet in the process, you would drag her down to your level!"

Cob paused and breathed slowly. "Ma'am. This is not a usual situation."

"That is an understatement. I can hardly agree to it."

"Mother! You promised!"

"I made no such assurances! This is beyond inappropriate. I won't have my daughter so shamed!"

Cob stood still, restraining every fibre in his body. Just then the door opened, and Rachel came bounding in with a smile, her hand flashing the ring on her finger. She stopped dead as the tension in the air crackled like lightning static.

"What is going on?"

Cob spoke up. "I've asked permission to marry..."

Rachel squealed with delight and ran over and hugged her sister, dancing her around. "You're getting married too? Oh, this is wonderful news! We can have a double wedding! I always thought that a double wedding was the most romantic thing ever, and with my sister. Oh Leah! This is perfect. We can have matching gowns and matching bouquets. I know some who prefer their own designs, but I really love the idea of matching... what do you think? But we could share the cake. Who needs two cakes for the same set of guests, and the same set of friends?" She talked hurriedly, her words falling over themselves in her enthusiasm.

Mr Leybourne raised his brow, and looked over at his wife, who frowned and scowled and shook her head, but without the same dogged resolve. She hadn't considered the prestige of a double wedding. "I don't know..."

Leah held up her hand and pushed Rachel away. "But they won't say yes. They won't give consent!"

"What? How? That is ridiculous! Why?"

"Because of... Cob... being a blacksmith and all..."

"Oh, pfft! Who cares? What I care about is that everyone is absolutely set on ruining my wedding day! Just when I get engaged and I think life is absolutely perfect, someone grabs a broom handle and jams it square into the spokes of my bicycle wheel. This is so unfair! You always try to spoil things for me, Leah!" She ran from the room. Walter held up his hand, but she had already flown past him in a whirl.

Leah ran after her calling out. "Rachel! It wasn't me! I tried to tell them..."

Cob stood in the middle of the room still holding the flowers. He put them on the table and shrugged awkwardly. "'Evening, Mr and Mrs Leybourne..." He turned slowly to go.

"Wait..." said Mr Leybourne. Cob turned back hopefully. "I have nothing against you personally, young man. It is just that we have standards... and it seems that..."

"It feels very personal to me, Sir. Good evening. Ma'am…" He nodded respectfully and he turned around and left.

As the door closed, Walter burst out laughing. "Well, I never! I could see from a mile away Leah would try that on for size. How could she not?"

"What do you mean, Walter?" asked Mrs Leybourne, now even more bewildered.

"I mean, a blind man could see that Leah is completely smitten with the smithy. Never seen her like that… all smiles and giggles and… oh, but all very appropriate of course," he quickly qualified. "But that girl is in love… beginning to end…"

"But she said very definitely that she wasn't in love; that she was after an adequate marriage."

Walter scoffed. "Well, of course. No one confesses to actually being in love! Take me and Rachel. She said yes, but it was completely understood that the coupling of our engagement is more like a stud farm than actual romance. Two solid blood lines coming together. It is much more appropriate to give the logical argument than a sentimental one. I thought it was a nice that Leah could have a chance to marry though. And Rachel seems taken with the idea."

"Are you recommending that we proceed with this appalling notion?"

"How many other offers has she had?" When they stared at him blankly, he said, "Without making too harsh a note of it, an older sister, unmarried, when the younger sister already is… that number will plummet even further. It is up to you of course… but I can't see how this will jeopardise her prospects, because, evidently, … she has none."

Mrs Leybourne stood to her feet in a hurry. "Wilhelmina! Wilhelmina!"

Billie came through the door and nodded a curtsy. "Yes, Ma'am?"

"Tell the girls to come down here... together. Immediately! We have something to discuss."

"Yes, Ma'am."

They came through the door, Rachel's eyes were red, and Leah looked like she wanted to throw up. They sat at the far reaches of the lounge from each other, sulky and sullen.

Mrs Leybourne nodded to her husband, and he cleared his throat. "We have discussed this... situation... further... with Walter. He is of the mind that it would be suitable for Leah to proceed with this engagement to Mister...?"

"Horne."

"Mr Horne. But it would please me most definitely, that if you have any doubts Leah, and if at any time, you want to withdraw from this engagement then please do so. Because once this is done... it is done."

"Oh, thank you Father! Thank you! That is what I am counting on. That is exactly what I am counting on!"

Both girls jumped to their feet, and exclaimed, and hugged, and danced, and smothered their father with kisses, and Leah formally thanked their mother for her leniency. Rachel thanked Walter for his influence, and then grabbed Leah's hand. "Oh, you will want to tell Cob this news! I am sure he will be greatly diverted that there is going to be a double wedding in the house!"

Walter stood there with a frown, and again raised his hand. "Double wedd... I never gave any consent to share my wedding day with a smithy!"

"Oh, don't be bothersome about this. We are going to have the best double wedding ever! We both want this here at home at Shipman Downs! You know of course that when you get back to the city, you will have a proper celebration anyway, in keeping with your society and position. Challenging two brides, even that might be too much for Walter Lincroft to take on."

Mr Leybourne sat down defeated, looking at Walter with a shake of his head. "I think she might be right about that, son. I think she might be right."

12

Rachel leant back against her pillows on her bed, as Leah sat at the dressing table, taking pins out of her hair. Rachel stared the play of the lamp light on the ceiling. "Do you know what annoys me? Father continues to beg you to change your mind if you have any reservations in marrying Cob, but I was never even once consulted on whether I even wanted to be married to Walter. Their double standards are showing; the hypocrisy of our family actually horrifies me. I have always been proud of my respectable family, but right now I'm exhausted by their insanity. This charade is driving me to distraction. And I have sunk to the lowest levels with them. Leah, how are we ever going to keep this pretence up? We have only two weeks left, but it feels like an eternity... and I am not sure I can sustain this ridiculous fascination and delight that I am supposed to have with Walter. I can't even remember the last time I had a decent conversation with Cob."

Leah pulled the loose hair out of her brush and looked at her sister in the reflection of the mirror. "Rachel, you have to do this, or the last time you spoke with Cob, *will* be the last conversation you ever have with him. You must not fade!"

"But..." Rachel considered her sister's calculated, unemotional frown on her forehead, as she sat her hairbrush down on the dressing table.

Leah picked up a sheet of paper and went back over her myriad of notes. "We have to just keep working through my lists. We must stay convincing... and keep checking off the items." Leah looked at the notes in her hand. "So, the final fitting for our dresses is tomorrow. Our veils still require some beading. It is well that we have heavy veils; even though the fashion is for filmy ones. It makes the sewing easier. Everything is identical... including the flowers, which need to be bulky... I might have Billie add some more greenery to the bouquets, just to be sure. Rachel. Don't give up. This is going to work. It has to. The only thing left to figure out is who will assist us in the swapping the certificates as we sign them. In the Shakespearian classic... the priest was the ally and collaborator of intrigue."

"Oh, Leah, are you suggesting we could we be as bold as Romeo and Juliet and talk to Reverend Reed? I am surely not convinced! It is so risky. I have absolutely no plan to end up dead like Romeo and Juliet. This is the most important detail of all."

Leah shook her head. "No, we can't approach him. Reverend Reed is entirely too conventional. He would denounce our plan as subversive, and condemn us to tradition," said Leah with all the analysis of a political commentator.

Rachel threw up her hands. "That's because it is! Deceitful and subversive to the core! I feel so guilty! Yet what are we supposed to do? Everything they have proposed is repulsive in its lack of consideration of us... as daughters... as women... and as potential wives. None of this makes sense! How can we assume that taking this course will correct the larger wrong? When will it ever come about, that we have the right to determine our own futures in straightforward ways?"

"Such a liberty is not within our reach... and even if by some social miracle it eventuates in the future, it is certainly not going to happen within this next fortnight. Rachel, we either do this... or we find our lives forever headed in a direction that is not of our choosing. It is not perfect – I know that. It could be... strictly speaking... considered morally wrong. But you have already acknowledged the other is not

right either. I know the argument that two wrongs don't make a right.
But what choice do we have?"

Rachel stared at Leah in despair. "We are doomed either way.
There is no straightforward alternative for us at all. I had no idea I could
stoop so low!"

"Rachel, to be frank, I don't know how to reconcile this any
other way than what Cob suggested. If we think of this as a parlour
game, while we sit at this card table, we are playing fair to achieve a
particular outcome. This way, we have a sliver of opportunity to
legitimately win, as much as any of the other players. So, the question
becomes: who is going to get the result they are playing for? I am
determined that we are going to play our hand to the best of our ability.
We will call their bluff right to the end; we will not table-talk; we will
not show our cards; nor will we give any indication that we have chosen
to engage in this game, in any other way than in the manner of
downtrodden women, just as they expect. So... we keep going. No one
is to know... not even Billie."

Rachel sighed and threw up her hands again. "Your level-
headedness prevails once more. We have invested too much. We
continue on... to create this sculpture into the shape that we want it to
be. And I have to keep believing that this sculpture will eventually be
positioned where it is destined to rest. That means you will have your
exciting metropolitan lifestyle... and I will be living with Cob out in my
Shipman Downs artist studio. It is to be expected that no one will
comprehend the desperately messy forming and shaping of this
artwork... or even appreciate the result. That is the lot of the artist I
suppose: to be perpetually misunderstood. I must focus on what I am
creating. I must adjust the light, and hammer the iron, and trust we

don't get burnt in the process. This is all that is left to do: to keep going on with the plan."

Leah picked up her brush again. "Yes, that... and finish the beading on our veils. We have to do that as well."

⁕

Rachel looked over the menu suggestions that her mother and sister had given her. This was a task they had allocated to her. Rachel knew this duty was less a matter of trust but was allowed because her mother considered that given her distractibility, she could not mess up something this basic. Rachel sighed. Again, Leah was the sensible ideal, even as a bride. Rachel really was not particularly invested in any of the meal options presented, and thought longingly of seared toast over a forge, with butter and rosella jam. How surprising it would be, if they served toast for the wedding reception, along with all the other toasts that were to be made in honour of the brides and grooms?

She found Billie in the vegetable garden pulling cobs of corn into a basket on her arm. Rachel looked at them wistfully. Cobs... She blinked and straightened up. "Do you have a moment, Billie? Mother and Leah wanted me to review the menu with you."

"Oh? For the wedding?"

Rachel nodded. She wished that Billie knew and understood what was going on. But she had vowed on her future, and her sister's future, and Cob's future... that no one else would be included in this circle of trust. Her face was sober, and her eyes misted as she thought about Billie's ongoing loyalty.

"Oh, Rachel, Honey, you don't seem so excited to be talking about roast meats and vegetables, or frothy deserts."

"Billie... to be honest... I am finding the preparations... exhausting. There is so much to think about."

Billie turned around and checked quickly to see if anyone was with in ear shot, and she put down her basket. "Rachel, Honey, is there any way you can extract yourself from this commitment to Mr Lincroft? I know you behave delighted and smiling when you are around him... but it seems to me that your heart is not in it."

"Oh, Billie... I know you are the one who notices what others don't even care to admit is really going on. But you must not say that. My parents have decided, and so we will proceed with the plan. Please... in this matter you have to trust that it will work out and try not to convince me otherwise. Otherwise, my resolve will melt completely."

"Honey, if somehow, I really believed I had that sort of influence, I would most decidedly try to divert you from this course. I cannot see how it will end any way, other than badly."

Rachel's eyes teared up. "Billie, I don't think you ever spoke a truer word. You understand more than you realise. This 'bad' ending is a very real possibility. But the cogs have started to turn... and it seems that the machinery of family politics rolls on regardless." Rachel wished that she didn't have to admit that she had more consideration from the paid staff, than her own parents... regardless of their stated good intentions. Sometimes intentions were so inadequate.

⁂

13.

Mrs Leybourne pinned up a stray hair and adjusted Leah's veil again around her spectacles. Billie fussed with Rachel's hem, and then handed them their bouquets, so gloriously full and generous that it hid the difference in their waistlines. Rachel took a deep breath. "Now mother, is the photographer ready at the bottom of the stairs to take our photo as we descend together? It is a very important shot."

"Yes, yes. He has his camera and stand all assembled."

"Please, go and check. I don't want this moment missed. Okay Leah, you lead the way... my wonderful older sister forges the way into matrimony."

Their mother nodded, teary. "Oh, my beautiful daughters... how wonderful you both look!" And Mrs Leybourne bustled out to check the photographer.

Rachel turned to Billie. "I love you, Billie. Thank you for all that you have done for me. Can Leah and I just have a moment... before we make this descent into matrimonial life?"

Billie nodded sagely and frowned. That sounded like the speech of a dying woman. She felt tears prickle her eyes... all the more because she knew Rachel's resolve to this course was a self-sacrificing act that meant she was condemned to never truly have the opportunity to happiness here-on-in. "As you will," Billie said, and she bobbed soberly as left the room.

The door closed; Rachel turned to her sister and nodded. Leah lifted her veil and passed over her spectacles. They swapped engagement rings. "Now we both have to get down the stairs blind. We have practiced with our eyes closed; now we have to do it with our eyes open. I can't see a thing with your spectacles on... and you can't see anything with them off. Are we ready?"

Leah took a deep breath and nodded. "I have never been more ready. We are doing this. You are now me... and I am you... so lead the way. I will ignore the irony that you still get to walk down the aisle first in spite of my huffing about my rights as your elder. Go slowly because I am following you."

Rachel stepped forward and stumbled slightly and adjusted Leah's glasses. She stood up, took a breath. "Righto. Here we go." They paused just before the bottom of the staircase, both graciously leaning on the banister, both smiling gloriously, unseen by the outside world through the density of their veils.

It was determined that it was too awkward to accommodate two brides on either side of their father, navigating the house, and narrow garden paths. So rather than have Mr Leybourne escort one daughter over the other, which was unsatisfactory to either of them, Mr Leybourne would meet his daughters at the altar to give them away. He stood with the grooms, who were waiting at the double bridal arbour in the garden.

Leah as the older sister, walked outside into the garden, down the aisle of arranged seating. Rachel followed after her. Their bridal processional seemed slow, almost like they were both feeling their way in the dark, and the musical recitation needed to be repeated. Twice.

Reverend Reed looked flustered. Of course, he expected brides would have any number of quirky preferences, so he had come to the pre-marriage meetings prepared to be the intermediary on just about every matter. In general, he had a policy of being accommodating without compromising the solemn sacredness of the occasion.

However, he had never done a double wedding before. Two brides and two grooms. The Reverend suspected that the only 'double' two brides would create, would be trouble, a double inclination for unpredictable, quirky problems.

One sober compromise that he needed to make was that the brides wanted their ceremony conducted outside the church. He didn't necessarily hold to the unyielding conviction of his peers, that a wedding could only be solemnised inside a Church, and it was always his preference to keep it within the chapel. But there had been some notable precedents set within the valley recently that challenged this tradition. According to his mind, those exceptions had been allowed to accommodate extenuating circumstances. However, in reality it had become the thin edge of the wedge, which had started an avalanche of this local trend of marrying outside the sanctuary of the Lord. Aside from the matter of the Church, he had been agreeably reassured how the family had negotiated most of their preferences beforehand. In fact, he had been pleasantly surprised that the sisters were notably of one mind and set on just about every matter.

Although a double wedding sounded like a practical solution – one ceremony for the family to manage in organisation and expense, with an emphasis on sisterly affection, in reality, the Reverend found the approach to the occasion entirely cumbersome. This observation was confirmed as he watched the brides walk unsteadily towards him across the uneven lawn. Everything about this double wedding was unconventionally identical. So very matchy-matchy: matching dresses; the same style shoes – allowing for the different heel height so that Leah was not shorter on the day; duplicate hair-styles; identical veils, and precisely corresponding floral bouquets. If it wasn't for some obvious differences, no one, and probably not even their parents, would have easily told the brides apart. The most obvious distinction was Leah's eyeglasses that were visible even through their heavy veils. Another was the enormous ring flashing on Rachel's finger, compared to the modest engagement ring Cob had placed on Leah's hand.

It was decided that the couples would serve as each other's witnesses: for simplicities' sake. Walter and Cob stood tall at the front of the bridal bower in the same cut of suit. Both men looked handsome and sophisticated in their matching suits, and it was generally agreed by the modest gathering of family and friends that no one would have been able to tell in that moment, which one of them was the illiterate blacksmith. There was a general unspoken consensus, that out of courtesy to the Leybourne's reputation, that it was appropriate to ignore the controversy of the second groom, and just to pretend for the duration of this ceremony that nothing was unusual. Time enough for sympathies after the wedding day when the harder realities of life settled in.

"Who gives these women to be married to these men?" The Reverend swallowed and coughed. Clumsy. That didn't even roll off the tongue properly. Mr Leybourne stepped forward awkwardly and gave his consent.

They said their vows in turn. *For better - for worse; for richer - for poorer; in sickness and in health...*

They exchanged their rings in turn.

At their insistence, the newly wedded couples were to sign the register and witness the entries, and then after being pronounced married they would share their first kiss as husband and wife. It was another point of "quirky". Leah had given a very convincing prudish argument that she didn't want to be kissed when she was not legally and legitimately married. There was a shuffle as grooms signed and witnessed their signatures. Then, as the brides rotated through the signing, an inconvenient gust of wind had the Reverend's pages of notes blowing across the lawn. It was all very confusing. Veils and skirts trailed around in a clumsy fog of tulle and lace. Reverend Reed broke out in a sweat. Finally, every section had a signature, and all legal matters were attended to. He took a deep breath and sighed. "Ladies and Gentlemen, it is with great pleasure, that I present to you Mr and Mrs Lincroft... and... Mr and Mrs Horne. Gentlemen, you may kiss your brides.

Up came the veils. Mrs Horne, squinting through her glasses, quietly reached up and took off her spectacles and passed them over to Mrs Lincroft, who stood beside her, and then proceeded to kiss her groom.

Walter paused, and grinned, indicated with a tilt of his chin. "See, I told you they were in love." Just then, he was taken by surprise as his bride quickly drew him in and gave him an equally passionate kiss. "Rachel, I... I had no idea that you... wow," he whispered. And he kissed her again. As he pulled back, he frowned. Leah quietly put on her spectacles and adjusted her veil.

Walter stared. "What... what is going on? You are not Rachel!"

Leah very quietly and firmly stated, "No. I am Mrs Walter Lincroft."

"I didn't marry you! This is outrageous! Rachel! What is going on?"

Rachel stood still, Cob holding her steady. She gripped his hand like a metal vice. Mr and Mrs Leybourne jumped to their feet.

Everyone started talking at once. Reverend Reed broke out into another profuse lather and dabbed his brow with the ceremonial stole around the shoulders of his ministerial robes. Then he stumbled over to a chair and sat down weakly before dizziness overtook him completely.

Eventually Cob looked down at Rachel and said with an amused grin, "Mrs Horne, are you able to shed light on this matter? There seems to be a great deal of confusion here."

Rachel shrugged and smiled, "I am pretty sure no one is listening to me just now. But just for your personal clarification, we are married." She smiled and reached up and kissed him again. "I am your wife, Cob Horne."

"Well, Mrs Horne," he said softly. "That is an interesting turn of events. Oh, how I love you..." And he kissed her forehead gently.

Mrs Leybourne shrieked. "Stop! Stop that! How dare you?"

"But Mother, we were just married. He is my husband. This is entirely fitting."

Walter stormed inside, and the bridal party followed him there. "What sort of mockery is this? I did not agree to any of this! You've deceived me into a precipitous marriage. I will have it annulled!"

Rachel stepped towards him. "You could...absolutely. But think about this logically, Walter. You have your third clause to consider. I will remind you of the very things that you considered valuable assets in a bride. These are all qualities Leah holds. Every single one of those attributes applies to her as well... some of them in greater measure. Since being in love was not one of the qualities you required, you are not out of pocket, Walter... but you could be, if you do not factor the practical implications of this arrangement. You now have a wife. She is beautiful, smart, more socially ept than me in every regard, and in spite of all my cautions, she declares that she loves you and is willing to tolerate your idiosyncratic whims. Perhaps most importantly, you have ticked the box needed to inherit: the point on which you told me on numerous occasions is your priority number one. This way, no one is humiliated or offended, and we all achieve our goals."

He looked over at Leah and swallowed. Of course, a handsome face was high on his list of attributes he wanted in a wife. Walter stared at Leah and thought she looked a little less odd in her pretty bridal make-up, even with her thick spectacle lenses. She was dressed identically in her bridal gown to the beautiful Rachel. He remembered her flirty little interaction with Cob in the Shepherds' hut and frowned thoughtfully. "I thought you were in love with the Smithy."

"From what I can see, I am certain you mean Rachel is in love with the Smithy. She is all over him, behaving quite like a bride in love."

He glanced their way, clutching at other like they were a life-buoy on a turbulent ocean, and then turned back to her and barely paused. "Huh. Of course, you understand it is appropriate that I would marry the *eldest* born daughter of a land baron..." He leant in and whispered. "Did you really have these feelings for me... like Rachel said?"

"I have the highest regard for you, Walter, and it has been that way since you first came to Shipman Downs six months ago. You just couldn't see me."

"Then tell me... what about the portrait sitting with the blacksmith? That didn't seem like you were thinking that way at all."

"Oh, but, Walter, I was. I was pretending Cob was you. You must know that I had you firmly in my sights right from the start. Rachel was completely right about one thing. You are much more handsome than he."

And he relaxed just a little and nodded. "I am reassured, Mrs Lincroft, that this could be a workable arrangement. I think my uncle will be pleased. But he must never know that I was not the instigator of this pretence. He must always understand that we masterminded this together as we recognised, against public opinion, that we are the more appropriate couple."

14.

The enthusiasm for a Bridal reception disappeared with the controversy of the wedding ceremony. Reverend Reed confirmed both couples were legally married if Walter Lincroft chose not to contest it. Then he excused himself and begged a bed to lay down, feeling too unwell to return to his parish manse in his current state. Mrs Leybourne was pale and briefly directed the serving staff to continue on with their duties as previously arranged. The affair was so misguided, and she couldn't reconcile the idea that Rachel had sacrificed such an opportunity with the purpose of staying at Shipman Downs. Her attempt to find a reasonable explanation suggested to herself that Rachel had been hoodwinked as much as Mr Lincroft.

Mr Leybourne took Walter and Leah aside to determine what was to be done. He found that Leah had her trunks packed to leave for the city. She reassured her father that she was determined to stay married to Walter Lincroft if he would have her... and Walter confessed to collaborating with Leah to engineer the whole affair. "Why didn't you just tell us that Leah was your preferred bride. It could have been arranged," he said quite bewildered.

"Mr Leybourne, I appreciate your reassurances, but the reality was that everyone expected Rachel to be my intended. And you know that if I could legally be the husband of two brides, I would have happily taken on that obligation. Sir, you must understand that I didn't want to break Rachel's heart or shatter Mrs Leybourne's expectations, however it was a difficult place I found myself to be. I have tried to resolve this in the most satisfactory way, but Leah is the person of my affections, and I couldn't let that go. I trust that Rachel finds a measure of comfort remaining here at Shipman Downs. She has always loved her home and perhaps that will be her consolation in this distressing situation."

That was quite a speech. Leah turned to him as they walked back to join the guests in the garden. "It is nice to think we have been collaborating in a forbidden love. It has the tone of all the famous great love stories."

Walter grunted. "Well, as of now, this is our story, Mrs Lincroft. Paste on your smile because we are a blissfully happy married couple."

"You forget one detail, Walter. This is entirely to my satisfaction, and no pretence is required on my behalf. I am completely devoted to you achieving all your ambitions. If you need to, consider this reception as practice for all the other audiences in your upcoming future who will need to be convinced that you have made a judicious choice. You can relax and enjoy the make-believe because I am having a marvellous time."

Walter considered her. "You know, Mrs Lincroft... I truly do believe this is very satisfactory."

Mr Leybourne sat Rachel and Cob down. "Rachel... my girl, you have pulled some stunts in the past, but I have to say... this is the most audacious one of them all."

Cob noted that Mr Leybourne did not hesitate to acknowledge Rachel shared a serious chunk of the responsibility in planning the intrigue of this situation. Rachel got up and gave her father a hug. He pulled back and held her at arm's length. "This is exactly why you wouldn't let me walk either of you to the altar. You knew I would be onto you and expose your ruse."

"Well, it has required some careful management of details..."

"Rachel, are you sure? Why didn't you say something?"

"And tell you what? That Mr Lincroft makes my skin crawl and that I am love with Cob? Not even you, Father, could have coped with such a turn on your expectations. No. It was better this way. Walter gets to take the credit. And I get to move out to the slab shack by the creek."

"Surely you aren't going ahead with the intention to live out *there?*"

"But that was the arrangement for Leah. If it was good enough for her, then Cob's plan has the same amount of merit for us. What a wonderful place to have a honeymoon year... or two... or a lifetime together. I think my point is not where... but together."

"But..."

"Oh, Father... I love Cob. Even scripture says *it is better to dwell in the wilderness, than with a contentious and an angry woman...* or man, as the case may be. This is better for me in every way."

He turned to Cob. "And you? What do you have to say for yourself, son?"

"Only what I said before. I love your daughter very much. I am a hard worker, and an honest person. I know we will have a happy life together."

"Honest? Were you speaking for Rachel, even then?"

"Most sincerely, Sir. Both your daughters are smart and strategic. You have done well with them, Sir."

"Humph. That is a matter that is up for debate. Devious and manipulative seems to be the order of today. Well, there seems to be nothing for it but to proceed."

"Sir?" said Cob, as Mr Leybourne sighed his resignation, and turned to leave. He paused and turned back around. "It was intimated that Mr Lincroft was going to have a private reception for his family and friends when he returns to the city. It gave me the idea that I would like leave to invite my family to celebrate our wedding also. A small gathering so that my mother can meet Rachel. Perhaps in a couple of weeks when the dust settles."

"You want us to accommodate them here at Shipman Downs?"

"Oh no, I think they would prefer to stay at Redwood Inn, and as a location, it is relatively close. But I just wanted to cover it out with you, in case you and Mrs Leybourne would like to attend."

"Well, Son, I think I am all weddinged out just now. Perhaps it would be better to let my nerves settle before I am introduced to my daughter's in-laws. But as far as your family goes... do what you think you must."

"Thank you, Mr Leybourne. I appreciate the consideration." And he held out his arm to Rachel and they went out to join the others for the wedding reception. It was an occasion in which Walter heartily took command of the proceedings, and he made a number of gloriously flowery toasts in honour of his bride.

✦❧✦

When the dinner was over, Walter and Leah left Shipman Downs in a coach for town. Leah had never looked happier. Cob took Rachel in the opposite direction, out to the Shepherd's Studio. He had set up a bedroom in the back corner of the barn. He carried her across the threshold of the studio, and as he put her down inside, Rachel gripped his hand and started to shake uncontrollably. "Oh Cob! Tell me it is true! Tell me it is over. Tell me we have escaped, and we are not condemned to a life apart."

He held her firmly, close to his chest so she could hear his heartbeat. "It is so. We are here. We are married. It is done."

Then, as if Rachel had been holding her breath for a hundred years, her breathing started to come in rasping, whooping gasps. Tears streamed down her face as she clung to him for dear life in the shadows of the studio. "Please promise me, Cob, promise you will not leave me. Promise me that you will see this through... 'til death do us part."

"Rachel, I made those vows, before God and witnesses. What makes you think I was not sincere in this? Of course, I will not leave."

"But you said it had to be in a church to be legitimate... that was the only way for us to be properly married."

"Well sure... if we could. My point was more about not running off into the fog to elope. A man of God married us. Your parents were there. These were the things that I thought were important."

"You don't think God judges our deception?"

"I think he would have preferred an upfront declaration... but life sometimes is not straightforward. Sometimes life is a complicated mess of rust and texture and tone... that takes form as it develops... like your sculpture. Sometimes it is misunderstood. And sometimes others don't appreciate the mangle of it all. Sometimes we go ahead and make the art-piece anyway, with flaws and mistakes... and work around the way it develops. You are an artist at heart, Rachel. You are the one who continues on carving out the shape and balance and style of your work with imagination. This has been what gives me hope, Rachel. I trust that God can use the sculpture of our marriage, even in the imperfections and the pounding of its forming."

He dried her eyes and led her further back into the shed to show her how he had set up their home while the wedding preparations were in full swing at the homestead. Rachel smiled at him and nodded. "Did I tell you, Mr Horne, that you look very handsome in your suit? You cut a very striking figure."

"As striking as a blacksmith working the forge... without a shirt... just braces?" He took off his suit jacket and hung it on a hook by the wardrobe.

"Definitely," she smiled. "I don't know anyone else who could carry both looks with such ease."

He nodded, rolling up the sleeves of his shirt. "I'm going to unhitch the cart and hobble the horse. Then I will be back."

She nodded, and smiled, and laid down on the bed. And when Cob returned from outside, Rachel was fast asleep, exhausted, on his pillow.

⁂

Cob stirred to the ring the smithy's anvil. He rolled over and saw Rachel, under the light of lanterns, still in her wedding dress, beating out a piece of steel. The sparks flew off in rhythm to her beating into the shadows. He sat up in bed and watched her, focused, and fully immersed in the act of creating. The stark contrasts of fine lace and heavy iron; white ivory and black soot; satin pleats and metal melds, were made boldly prominent by the vitality of her motion. He had a front row seat in a concert hall. His sense of amazement and wonder almost overwhelmed him with the complexity of composition she was weaving. It struck him just then, that his wife was an artwork from the creative hand of God... and perhaps it would take years of study to comprehend the nuances of play between line and shape; tone and colour; pattern and texture; balance and form... that made up this masterpiece.

Rachel paused and wiped her brow. She glanced up and saw Cob sitting on the side of the bed in a relaxed sort of slouch, watching her intently. "How long have you been awake?" she asked quietly.

"Long enough to see you know how to dress up for an occasion and that nothing will stop you from working on what you love, to see it more complete... more whole." He came over to her and handed her a mug of water he had picked up on the way. She took a drink, and he smiled with affection.

"You don't judge me for that. That's refreshing," she said as she set down the mug, and picked up the rod she had been working on and doused it in the water barrel.

He raised his brow and grinned. "Although that may be the case, I'm not going to presume that Billie will be as accommodating when she tries to launder your dress, Mrs Horne."

"I have a confession to make, Mr Horne," she said looking at him seriously.

"Really? Should I be worried?"

"I'm not sure. The truth is... I think I have a crush on the Smithy."

"But I heard you declare, in this very same studio, that such a thing was impossible... quite inappropriate."

"Yes, I did say that... but I think, that unlike my sister, it is established that I have a taste for the misunderstood, and the inappropriate."

"Perhaps it is fitting then, that I also disclose that have a serious thing going for the artist of this studio. It seems my heart is in her hands... the way that she works, and forms, and holds... suggests to me that my fate is destined to be moulded by this artisan." He lent forward, pressing her back against the sculpture. She dropped the steel in her hand, and it clattered loudly to the floor in the pre-dawn stillness, as she entwined her arms and her heart around him.

16.

They walked up towards the Redwood Inn reception area, Uncle Jac walking slowly to join them for this family reception. Years ago, this prestigious homestead had been converted to wayside inn accommodation. Cob alluded to family history here, and Rachel was curious about the connection, but her questions were smothered by a woman rushing towards them.

"Oh, Theodore! You are here!"

"Mother..." Cob enveloped his mother in a hug.

She pushed him back at arm's length and gave him a maternal scan. "Look at you. Already married! I couldn't believe this news. Married life seems to agree with you, my son."

He grinned. "It does. Mother, this is my wife... Rachel. And Rachel... let me introduce you to my mother, and also my Godparents, Uncle Ruben and Aunt Abby."

Callie embraced Rachel in an enormous hug. "Oh, Rachel! How lovely to meet you, and oh, it is so good to have you as part of our family! And look, Abby, see how elegant she is! Such pretty hair. How Theodore's father would have loved to have met you."

"Mum... please. Don't overwhelm her with all of that."

"All of what? My son is married! Now we have a daughter! This is something to celebrate! They make such a handsome couple, don't they, Abby? Oh Jac, I am glad you were able to take Theodore on at this time. What good luck for all of us!" His mother took her brother's arm and led him aside, enquiring after his health.

Rachel took advantage of the pause and also pulled Cob aside, with the suggestion of an urgent enquiry. "Theodore? Your mother calls you *Theodore?*" she whispered with a delighted smirk of amusement.

"She's the only one. And I would prefer you didn't start."

"Oh, I don't know... it sounds so very cultured. Theodore-the-Smithy. It almost has a classic medieval ring to it."

"How I wish, that just now, I had something to pull out to entice some respectable social manners from you... but I have nothing. So, I am just going to have to beg your good-will on this."

"Begging? That also has an appealing ring to it," she said with mischief in her eyes.

"Please behave. She is my mother."

Rachel nodded and smiled and made her way up the stairs to the verandah of Redwood Inn where the others had settled into a casual circle around the table drinking tea. "Cob was telling me that there is a shed by the creek at home, that has particular significance in your family."

"Oh yes! It really does. The Shipman Down's shed! Theodore was born there. Not the most congenial of circumstances I must admit, but all is well that ends well. And I have to say, I could not be prouder of the man Theodore has become. Exactly how a mother should feel when she sees her child doing well."

"How incredible that Cob now lives and works at Shipman Downs. What a wonderful sense of symmetry that has."

Cob cut in. He was thankful that Rachel had avoided the obvious observation that they were actually living *in* that barn, and he quickly changed topics. "Uncle Ruben... are you still working in the administration offices?"

Uncle Ruben gave some general observations about the pending move towards Federation, as they were anticipating that Queen Victoria would soon sign the Royal Commission of Assent. Rachel raised her brow. So, this was *that* uncle. She leant over and whispered behind her hand. "Cob, is this your uncle... the one who is a clerk; not a felon?"

Cob spluttered in his drink. How did Rachel get the idea that his uncle was a common clerk? Well, now was not the time to correct that detail. They were here to enjoy a family occasion, not top-note accomplishments. Uncle Ruben may be his Godfather, but in reality, after his father died, he had taken on a closer, more significant, role. Cob still felt the sting of Ruben's disappointment that he had abandoned the legal professional path. Cob took Rachel's hand and tried to keep his tone light. "Not everyone in our family is listed as wanted, some of us are quite respectable."

"Respectable is reassuring." Did that mean if Cob was respectable, the others present were not? Were they really lawbreakers, wanted by the Law? Is this why he didn't talk much about his family?

Aunt Abby was close enough to hear their exchange and she smiled with practiced refinement. "Oh my. Young Rachel, I don't think you have been given an accurate picture of the background of whose son you have fallen in with. This family has quite a colourful history. Cob's father was given all sorts of warnings regarding his involvement in the shearers protests against automation. Ted was as fiery as his hair was red. I think it would please Ted that you both have that same quality. His involvement pushed him into hiding for a time. Ruben here, also had his face on posters for embezzlement, bushranging, and kidnapping, and spent time in prison. Now he continues to get people off-side at all levels of society. It seems you have tumbled into a hereditary pool of political stirrers and social discontents."

Rachel swallowed and her smile melted to a frown as she took another sip of the very expensive wine in her glass, with a shake of her head. Aunt Abby sounded amused that Cob's family was grounded in protest, corruption, crime, and penal incarceration. Did his family have no scruples at all? The contented, smiling respectable group before her, toasting the happiness of their favourite son, belied any impression of agitators and delinquents this woman declared they were. But Rachel was quite sure, by the style of these ladies' fashionable gowns, the cut of Uncle Ruben's suit, and the quality of the leather that made his boots, that they were definitely overreaching on a clerk's wage. Is that why Cob had taken particular effort to dress well for this occasion?

Rachel had expected to meet a relatively clean, if shabby family, and she had been so determined to be kind and generous in her conversation with them. But this was completely not what she expected. Aunt Abby had given her the simplest explanation: they had come by their money through immoral and illegal means. Clerk, Uncle Reuben may be, but she would bet her bottom pence that there was also a fair smattering of 'felon' in his curriculum vitae, required to fund such a lifestyle. It sounded like this godfather was indeed the head of one of those disreputable crime families. Of course, he would sponsor Cob through university. He was not a lowly clerk discharging his responsibility of support out of a spirit of sacrifice, as Cob had relayed the story, but he was obviously hoping to use the next generation to create a legal net around their dubious activities. If they disclosed in that moment, they were drinking bootleg together, and had access to all sorts of other contraband, she would not have been surprised.

Rachel felt a great wave of unease expand across her chest. What if she had made a terrible mistake by marrying Cob? What if, instead of avoiding the monotony of social respectability, she had ended up in the bottom of a barrel with some very rotten apples? She had been beguiled by Cob's charms and smooth civilised talk, disguised in the warm glow of the metal that she loved. Was this now what her life was to be? Protecting her family's name from being soiled by association with a pack of lawbreakers and delinquents? She thought she knew him, but as Cob's mother enthused over son's good looks and Rachel's charms, she wondered how much she really knew him at all. Aunt Abby spoke gracefully in her elegant gown with a persuasive smile, and it seemed to Rachel she had been deceived... far more than the veil that hid her sister's face who stood before Reverend Reed beside Walter Lincroft.

⁂

It was a relief to go home. Home. She silently got down from the cart and went straight to work on her sculpture. This, at least, was something that was real and reliable. The furrows on her forehead deepened as she struck and slammed the iron on her anvil. She turned the iron; over and over; rotating and pounding; rotating and pounding.

Cob stood at the door watching the intensity of her frenzied work. This was not the focused creativity he was used to. This was frenetic, emotional, feverish. He was confused. He had honestly thought Rachel would love his family, and that they would get along together like a house on fire. The only fire here, was where the coals were being blown white by the bellows in the forge furnace.

He walked over to her. "Rachel? What's going on?"

She didn't pause. She didn't acknowledge him. Rotate and pound. Rotate and pound.

"Rachel!"

She stopped and put down her hammer. "What?" she said impatiently.

"What happened?"

"Nothing. I don't know what you mean. We had the private reception as we agreed. I have now met your family, and they have met me."

"Yes... but now it seems you have decided to execute your sculpture by a hundred and forty lashes. Why are you beating up on it so?"

"You lied to me!"

"I'm sorry, what?"

"You lied to me. You make out you are a clean-cut, unassuming, wholesome-living man who works with his hands. But you are not! You simply are not!"

"What are you talking about? Are you disturbed that my family has money? Yes, they would have preferred a different profession than blacksmithing for me. I explained that. I am still me."

"I think my parents are right. I am trapped in a marriage that is completely unsuitable. How could I have ever thought that this would work?"

"You knew what you were getting by marrying me. I never pretended to be something I am not."

"But that is exactly my point, Cob. Exactly! I didn't know! My deception has come back to bite me! I convinced myself it was a clever ruse, but instead I become the victim of a deception that will forever hang over me as this veil of shame.”

“Rachel, why don’t you sit down? You seem quite overwrought.”

“Don’t treat me like my mother! I am fine. Completely fine! However, I will not be drawn into your designs. I absolutely will not!”

“Rachel? You are judging me... for what? Being a blacksmith? I told you why I didn’t take the professional track. How can you judge me for that when you do what you do?”

“If you were a family of blacksmiths, I would be relieved.” She may have previously declared she had a taste for the misunderstood, and the inappropriate, but she had never intended to be married into a reprobate family who took pride in their moral squalor, while dressing up and putting on a face of respectability. This was not what she meant at all. Oh no, not this. Not at all!

✢✢✢✢✢

17.

Long hours at the Shipman Downs' blacksmith workshop became the norm as Cob started taking on the weight of Jac's workload. Uncle Jac became less and less able to hold the heavy hammer or beat steel welds. Even without any formal acknowledgement of a changeover, they had effectively switched roles. Cob was doing most of the work of the senior smith now, and Jac generally watched from a chair where he sat in the corner and gave Cob a few tips on the thornier problems encountered in the job. Sometimes Cob would look over to find him dozing, or at other times, he seemed so pale and still, that he hardly knew if he was still with them.

Late one afternoon, Cob was working by the anvil, relinking chains that were used with the draft-horses to de-stump the clearing paddocks. Cob looked up to see Uncle Jac stand up and start towards him, but before he got very far, he wavered and collapsed on the floor of the shed. Cob bundled him into his cart and took him home to the Shepherd's Studio. Rachel helped support his weakening frame inside and assisted him to lie down on their bed. Cob drew her aside. "Rachel, I know you don't regard my family well, but I would really have Uncle Jac looked after out here, rather than being in his own hut alone. Is that something you might do... for him? He can't manage on his own anymore, and I can't do care for him and work the blacksmith shed as well.

"Cob, you know I regard Smithy Jac well. Of course, he stays here. Of course."

"I'll retrieve his things from his hut... his bunk and bring them out. Thank you, Rachel. I appreciate this very much."

Cob sent some of the station hands out to deliver Jac's things. They carried in his gear, and Rachel set up an area for him. He had his bunk and washstand, his favourite mug and chair. Rachel manoeuvred a divider into place for a little privacy, made up his bed with clean linen, and by the time Cob came in after dark, Jac was settled in, sleeping.

Cob sat down at the table, and Rachel served his meal. But rather than their uncomfortable silence, leaving him to eat alone as she usually did, she made a coffee and sat down opposite him.

He nodded. Tired.

"He had some chicken soup. He's been sleeping a lot, even though I can tell he is in pain. Even when he does doze off, he is muttering and wincing and flinching... all the time."

Cob nodded. "He is past pretending that this is going away. I'm reckoning that he doesn't have long."

"I have to stay here with him, but I have written a note to Mother, to have a doctor sent out. He may have some elixirs to help settle the pain. If you could drop it off at the homestead tomorrow..."

"Yeah. I will. Put it with my lunch satchel. I'm beat so I'm going to turn in. Thanks Rachel. This kindness is appreciated." Cob dragged himself to his feet, washed up briefly, and was asleep, almost before his head hit his pillow.

Rachel sat for a time, drinking her coffee. She stared at Cob asleep on their bed and wondered what she had allowed to happen here. She shook her head and stared vacantly at her sculpture that stood like a rusty monument to unfinished dreams. She couldn't remember the last time she worked on it as a labour of love. Once she couldn't wait to attend to it; now it was an effort. And mostly the effort was too much, so she didn't bother. She filled her days, looking after the chooks, or the vege garden, or cooking, or washing, or mending. Stale, uncreative, monotonous. She felt her life had shrivelled like the apple core she found withered in the corner of the studio. It was so dry that even the mice had scorned it.

In the morning when she woke, Cob had already left. This was their life. How do you co-exist without seeing the other person? How do you live around someone without ever connecting with them? She was hanging out the washing when Uncle Jac emerged looking around. "Smithy Jac! Good morning."

His grey beard was as scruffy as his grey eyes were gentle. "So, this is the castle that Cob tells me about? Think he may have exaggerated its comfort somewhat."

"Did you sleep okay?"

He shrugged. "Better than I have for a month of Sundays. Could be the pretty bed-sheets. Maybe that's the luxury Cob was talking about."

Rachel finished pinning the last of the laundry to the clothesline and picked up her basket. "I doubt Cob ever said such nonsense. Are you ready to try some breakfast?"

They walked inside and sat down. Uncle Jac declined to eat, although he took the mug of tea that Rachel offered him. "Smithy Jac. I've sent for a doctor."

"Huh. A doctor's not going to be able to do squat. You and me both know that."

"Perhaps. Still, if he can prescribe something for the bad days, I will be comforted, even if it means nothing to you. Please, try to eat something. Please..."

"Well, I don't feel like eating. But... perhaps I could... if..."

"If? If what? Please. Anything."

"Well... okay. A trade. I'll try to eat if you answer me a question. I reckon I could give some of that soup you had yesterday another go."

"That is an easy deal! As long as you eat first." And she quickly heated him some broth before he changed his mind.

He ate slowly and she monitored every spoonful. He forced himself to keep going to the bottom of the bowl. He put down his spoon and belched. "Now. My question."

Rachel nodded.

"Why haven't you finished that monstrosity? You should be done by now."

"Oh. The Shipman Downs project. It hardly seems to have a point anymore. I try every so often... but I just do not have the energy. Married life is more demanding than perhaps I anticipated."

"Huh. Mrs Rachel Horne. Never took you for a fraud."

"What are you talking about? I was genuine in what I said! I cannot force the art. It has to be inspired."

"Wasn't talking about the sculpture. And you know it."

"Smithy Jac! I am not the one who has *not* been forthright."

"You keep telling yourself that. It will make this palace that Cob loves so well, all the more cosy for it." And he stood up and went outside, sat in his old squatter's chair that was put out there for his comfort; and he slouched against the rattan back with a cushion and smoked his tobacco pipe, grimacing through the pain.

Rachel finished her cup of tea with frown on her brow. When Smithy Jac came back inside after a while, he laid down, and was soon asleep. When he got up, he looked sort of sheepish. "Can't account for it... never been a napper. Perhaps it was all that time looking at the rafters last night."

"You told me you slept well," she accused.

"Said I slept better here than at the other place. It all depends how you look at it..."

"Hmm. Well, it is quite late. What do you want for lunch? More soup?"

"So, you are out to fatten me up... like a prize bull. I doubt your best efforts will manage it though."

"*I* doubt you will let me."

"I'll give the soup a go... but only if I get another question."

"Uncle Jac. That is not playing fair."

"I'm dying. I don't have to play fair anymore. It is my only pleasure left. That, and my pipe."

She frowned. "I may well be caught in a trap made by my eagerness to have you eat something. Very well," and she served him a small portion in his bowl and sat down with her tea opposite him.

He stopped a couple of times, and Rachel smiled. "It seems I don't have to worry about your interrogation after all. Well, that is a relief." He held up his hand and forced himself to keep going to the very last spoonful. Rachel shook her head. "You must really want that question."

He sighed from his marathon exertion and put down his spoon. "I want to know... what happened... at that Redwood reception. You arrived as honeymooners... and left a staid, old couple, who could barely tolerate each other. Something happened."

"I met Cob's family."

"My family..."

"Well, I certainly don't put you in the same rotten barrel with them. I have known you for longer. I trust you."

"What are you talking about? My sister is twice the person I am."

"It was more the association with the others. Mr and Mrs Davey. I was disturbed by their familiarity, and Cob's association with them."

"Rachel, you grew up at Shipman Downs. I know it is not upper-class, regardless of your relatives' best efforts, but you have sufficient confidence to hold you own with types like the Daveys. You did okay."

"Why would I be intimidated by their ill-gotten money? I would never stoop so low!"

"I'm not a fan either, but Davey is a man who has made a difference. And to his credit, he didn't rant on about the Federation effort. It was a relief not to be subjected to all that political mumbo-jumbo during a family shindig. In some circles, it's all you hear."

"Politics? What are you talking about?"

"Davey... that's what he does. He's in politics."

"Oh, I didn't realise he was clerking to high-profile figures. Not that it makes any difference to me. I have *never* seen a clerk wear boots like that! That has got to be telling how a man lines his pockets."

"Cob told you he was a clerk? The man isn't a clerk. He *has* clerks."

"No... that was not what..."

"He works as legal and advisory counsel to all sorts of big wigs... done so for years. Most recently he's been working on the move to

Federation. The man's a lawyer. An influential one, which is surprising since he is as honest as any man who ever lived by bread."

"He's a *lawyer?*" she gasped incredulously. "Then why would he misrepresent himself as a clerk? That's hardly *honest.*"

"Never heard him ever tell anyone he's a clerk. Just an honest poli'. Yeah, I know. You wouldn't think that those two go together, but the man is a straight shooter. Over the years, that one feature has got him off-side with all types... many times... got him in all sorts of hot water over the years. And yet it is like he is made out of that Indian rubber compound. He just keeps bouncing back."

"But Aunt Abby... at the reception dinner she spoke about being..." Rachel shook her head. Confused.

"Ahh... the bushranger thing. Yes well, that did actually happen. He was exiled for a time. He lived up in the hills behind Redwood, but he was cleared of all the charges they tried to pin on him."

"Vindicated? He is not... Why would she go to such lengths to tell me he was on wanted posters?"

"Huh. Who knows? She's always telling that story. It's become her favourite parlour yarn. You know... we all have an anecdote to pull out to brighten up family occasions. Those types of stories are about how we get to where we are. You... me... even this place, Shipman Downs... we've all got our stories."

"Stories? How would we even know what those stories are?"

"Good point, I guess. Unless someone tells them... we can end up making assumptions about how we get to where we are. Davey blew the whistle on a fair swag of rotten practices after he was cleared. There is always a Red-Reform happening somewhere... it is like his middle name. And he continued to have the attention of the powers that be.

Don't know the ins and outs of it... but I do know they have stood by Callie and Cob all the way through... particularly after Ted's accident."

"Cob's father? What happened?"

"Cob was just a little ankle-biter. Terrible unlucky affair, but nothing sinister, which is kinda ironic given how Ted could sniff out a problem without any effort. He nearly died after a beating from that Shearer's affair. Abby saved his life by getting his wounds tended properly. In the end, Ted's horse was spooked by a snake and he busted his neck in the fall. Nasty business. Broke Callie's heart being widowed so young. Pulled out of it eventually, but she never married again. And yet Abby never left her side. Those Davey people have been good to them. Cob counts them family. As do I."

"But... she said..." Rachel's eyes filled with realisation.

"You thought what she said about all that history, was a full confession of an ongoing life of crime?"

"Bushranging, kidnapping, arrests and agitation... she said it all so seriously!"

"No accounting for some people's sense of humour I guess," Jac said with a shrug.

"I know there is no possible way a clerk could afford the manner in which they were living. I thought..." She stared at him hard.

"Suppose they came outfitted for an important family event. Never seen them put on airs though."

"Oh, Smithy Jac! What have I done?" She stood up and ran outside.

Jac let her be. He poured himself a mug of tea and took it outside, sitting in the squatter's chair as he lit his pipe. He dozed off and woke to the ring of the double bounce strike of hammer against anvil. That sound reminded him of church bells... a call to gather; a declaration announcing something important. He smiled to himself and tapped out his pipe, filled it again and lit it, looking at the smoke swirl out towards the trees along the creek. It felt peaceful here, and he was grateful. If he had to go out... then what better place to go out, than where his nephew came in.

But there was one matter on which he was determined he would see through. If the Good Lord would allow it, he would not go until he knew that this standoff he was witnessing, was reconciled. Spats he understood, but at least they should be based on more information than this mishmash of misunderstanding. Perhaps another story needed to be told.

He got up and went back inside. He winced and steadied himself by the door. Rachel looked up and quickly put down the iron tongs in her hand. "I'm sorry for disturbing you. I forget myself..."

"Naa... The sound of the anvil... it's like a babe's lullaby for me. You keep working while I lay down. It's a comfort." And he was right. He was soon asleep again.

⁂

18.

Cob stood at the door when he came home. He didn't quite know what to make of it. He hadn't seen Rachel working on her sculpture since... since a long time. He looked at her standing over the anvil. Here was an echo of a past passion and his heart ached as he watched her and listened to the metal strike against metal. He had promised he would stay, and he intended to keep his word to his last dying breath... but he wondered if he would be so devoted to his work in the blacksmith shed if their relationship was different. Jac came up beside him and stood with him as he watched. Cob didn't even turn his head when he spoke. "You told me once, Uncle Jac, that this was a dead end... destined for heart break. I gotta admit I reckon you were right."

"Huh," said Uncle Jac. "I was counting on you proving me wrong. Wouldn't be the first time."

"When have I ever proved you wrong? Never have."

"I told your mother I didn't need to be baby sat. Didn't want any smart-arsed kid coming to look after me. But you came anyway, with that cock and bull story that you needed more instructing... and here you are. You and my stubborn sister made a move. And right now... I am grateful you did. This is what I needed. You proved me wrong."

Cob had not moved his eyes off Rachel. "Jac... I just don't understand what happened. I don't get it. I don't..." His voice faltered and he swallowed hard.

"Perhaps she doesn't get it either. Don't give up on her yet mate. Seems to me she is pounding through some stuff now. Something has been sitting on her heart like brittle slag and she is beating it off.

Can't make anything worthwhile without a bit of heat and hurt. It doesn't matter what we make, there is always some hammerscale flaking off. It is part of the process."

"But..."

"Just you be ready when she is ready. Don't shut her down. I'm going to bed." And he walked over to his bunk, breathless from the exertion. This time he did take some drops of the elixir left by the doctor.

Cob watched her in the shadows, sparks flying as she struck the iron in her hand. He didn't want to move, and he didn't want to interrupt the flow of her making. He liked the idea she was back at it. It felt familiar, and the familiar felt like hope. The movement of Jac settling into his bunk caught her eye, and she looked up. She glanced over at the door, and she saw Cob standing there watching. "How long have you been there?" she asked.

"Long enough to see you haven't lost your touch. It is good to see you forging again..."

She stared at him for a bit, and put down her hammer, and brushed her hair up out of her eyes, streaking black through the red. "I have made your dinner. I should stop now anyway. Jac needs to rest, even though he has told me that beating the anvil is his lullaby."

"Well, lucky for me, I don't need rocking or a lullaby. Thanks for dinner." He washed up, rubbing his face and arms with a rough towel, and sat at the table as Rachel put his meal down. He looked up at her and swallowed. The flickering lamp light made it look like her hair was on fire. He indicated the chair. "Umm... you could sit. Tell me how Jac was today."

She hesitated and then sat down. "Well... nothing seems too different. He has moments when he seems like his old self... and then at other times, I am so frustrated because I don't know how to help him. The mixture the doctor left... he doesn't like to take it. He's not eating much... but I have been bribing him, so he is at least taking some soup."

"Bribe? Never known Jac to be swayed into corruption," he said with a tired grin.

She blinked. There was that theme of integrity again. Accused without cause.

"What do you have that would give you that much leverage?" he asked studying his meal.

She shrugged as if his question was the most normal thing. "I have the means to satisfy his ungentlemanly kind of curiosity. He wants to ask me questions."

"About what?"

"My sculpture... things like that..."

"Oh." He didn't know what else to say. This was awkward, uncomfortable, and frightening. Terrifying actually. Jac's raspy voice was still strong in his ear: *Don't shut her down. Be ready.* He swallowed. "It seems like you have done a bit on it today. When do we get to move it into place?"

"When will it be finished? Oh. Not for a while yet, I don't think." She smiled faintly. "You still believe."

He gave another tired grin and tried to keep his tone light. "Well... it could be my unwavering faith in your skill to accomplish the project... or it could be the fact that it is now clogging up our living room... and it would be good to have it done."

"It may take longer now. I've decided to change it..."

"Oh? How?"

"Rather than just a ship... I am making it into a storyboard of our family... the story of Shipman Downs... like those old-fashioned story boxes... with the carved figures all around the sides, that tell of some myth or legend or folktale as you turn it around."

"Huh. I've heard of quilts like that... telling family history, embroidered into the panels."

"Yes, like that. Three masts... three generations... and I want to make figures and shapes embedded into the textured iron sides... not obvious, but if you look, you can see the stories of Shipman Downs for each of those generations. Not just my grandfather coming here... but a record of other family events. I've starting to collate the stories in my head, and I've done some sketches in my book. The shepherd's hut burning down in the bushfire; Mother and Father's wedding; the kidnapping; your birth; the record wool clip year; me getting stuck up the windmill as a kid; learning blacksmithing from Smithy Jac and making the studio... our double wedding..."

She took him over to the frame and showed her where she had started. "This is the beginning... my grandfather's honourable discharge from the Queen's navy."

Cob shook his head amazed. "You have taken something that was very good... and just made it brilliant. You are extremely clever, Mrs Horne."

She looked at him... and frowned. "Cob..."

"Yes...?"

"I don't think I have been clever about something... something important..."

"What do you mean?"

"I mean us... I have spent more time on this sculpture today... than I have on the sculpture of our marriage since we came here. You said when we married that I wouldn't stop working on what I love, to make it better... but I haven't done that. I have not been fair. I didn't give you a chance. I didn't tell you why I was scared. I wouldn't let you say anything because I thought you would defend your family over me."

"Why does it have to be one over the other? Can't it be possible to love in two places at once? I love my family, Rachel. I do. And I don't want to lose them. But I don't want to lose you either. I love you Rach... Oh I really do."

"I feel like an idiot. Jac told me your uncle Ruben... is a lawyer."

"Yeah so? I told you that... remember? I said he wanted me to follow in his footsteps. That's why he organised that trial job as a legal clerk. He's still disappointed I didn't go ahead with it."

"See... I think... I thought it would be impossible that anyone would choose this... over a profession like that. So, I heard... in my head... what I heard was that he was just a small-time clerk... so that the gap between there and here wasn't that big."

"Huh. So? Does it matter what he does? Most people don't like politicians anyway."

"Well, it did for me... because then something important didn't add up..." and she went on to explain her assumptions about the family living outside the means of a lowly clerk, even if he was clerking for some professional lawyer.

Cob shrugged. "Well, it's not the first time he's been falsely accused. He told me once it comes with the territory. Perhaps that is part of what scared me off. I saw what people put him through when there was no fault to be taken. Guess I figured I didn't need to put myself through that. Seems it has happened anyway."

"Cob, I am so sorry. I thought this was my punishment for choosing to marry the way we did. That the deceiver became the deceived. I believed this is what I had to live with."

"Rachel? When are you going to forgive yourself for marrying me? Am I such a poor choice?"

"Poor? Oh Cob. No! You don't understand. I thought you were above that kind of life. I was angry that even though you may have extracted yourself from their criminal clutches by coming here to be with Smithy Jac, that at some point they would embroil you in their reprobate life of corruption again. I didn't want you feeding into their lifestyle."

"So, your answer was to shut me out? Rachel, we are answerable to our own choices. Even if what you thought was true, surely there is a way we can work through this together. Together is what I promised, regardless – better or worse; rich or poor; sick or well. Together..."

"I guess I understand that more now. I have been thinking about how you work so hard. Dawn to dark. I'm reckoning that if you had money in the background that would make your life easier... why would you do it this way? Why would you live here, with me, like this? Yet you have never wavered. Father is extremely pleased with your work."

"Your father might be okay with my work, but he is still not pleased I married his daughter."

"Ahh... but I have a plan. A plan that will see you as the favourite son-in-law in a very short time."

"Rachel? Last time you had a plan... and pulled it off... I got what I wanted. I did get to marry you. And yet I have ended up sleeping alone... and eating alone... and I miss you so much. I don't want to keep doing it that way. I want to do our life together. Please consider what you are thinking about."

"You miss me?"

"Desperately..."

She stepped forward and smiled. "It merely involves another dinner invitation... so my family can meet your family. Simply, it would mean some serious fashion parading and some heavyweight name dropping. My mother and your mother will end up best friends... and you will be her favourite son-in-law."

Cob shook his head as he took off his shirt and hung it on a hook by the washstand. He poured warm water into the bowl from the stove. "I have no need to be any one's favourite, other than yours," he said as he washed.

"Oh, but you are. Cob, you are. I have missed my husband too."

"I've spoken to your father about having an apprentice; and maybe another offsider as well. The station has too much work for just one smith, now that Jac is not working. Perhaps that would ease the hours some. I could be home more..."

She nodded, encouraged. "And then... if I made an occasion of the installation of my sculpture when it is finished, we can invite all your family out here. It would seem such a natural way to explore some of the wonderful circles of society they circulate in."

He shook his head and smiled as he hung up the towel. "Aunt Abby would be telling all her artesian friends. She is a very good marketer of other people's passion."

"See, this would be a very astute plan for an upcoming artist."

Cob reached over and pulled Rachel to his side. "Would this astute plan of yours mean I get my wife back? Because if it does not... I am not tempted to collaborate in your manoeuvring and scheming in anyway."

Rachel looked up and nodded. "Oh yes. I'm so sorry, Cob. Please forgi..."

"Forgiven," he murmured as her words were smothered in his kisses.

⁂

Epilogue

The marquee stood on the lawn. Tables were scattered around the trees with white cloths. Mrs Leybourne was running to and fro, in a flurry of anticipation, anxious to meet the special names who were about to arrive. Aunt Dorothea had filtered through the guest list and had already determined which influential patrons Felix, and the newly wed Gwendolyn and her husband, were to fortuitously bump into. She stood under the trees, coaching them again in the spontaneous social graces required to support her quest.

Aunt Abby was supervising the placement of the easels in the pavilion and where the various canvases, sculptures and figurines were to be arranged in this portable gallery. Special guest artists were given a slot in the program to talk about their part of the exhibit. Rachel's ship sculpture was the largest piece displayed, and it stood centre stage on the lawn with a series of mounted posters placed around the base, retelling the depicted stories of Shipman Downs history. Each wrought-iron mounting frame was an art piece in its own right. Aunt Abby had arranged for a book to be published as a souvenir of the occasion, and a table was set out with the books displayed. Invited honoured guests were given a complimentary copy, signed by all the artists on their featured page; others could purchase their copy. The stringed quartet, quiet and classic, created a backdrop of elegance to the lawn party, as ladies and gentlemen began to arrive, gliding through the exhibits.

Leah and Walter were bemused by all this fuss about Rachel's foray into sculpture, but they put a good face on it in the light of the splash made by genuinely recognisable influential names. Cob's mother hovered around, in her official role as Aunt Abby's assistant, showing guests where they could eat, or obtain their drinks, or which part the planned sequence of the program was about to begin. The whole day had a wonderful festive feel, lacking the rough, thrown-together, backyard reputation that city folk assume they will be subjected to, if they have to ride their coach further than an hour out of town.

Uncle Ruben opened the event on behalf of the Leybourne's hospitality at Shipman Downs. He read a letter from the Prime Minister's office about the value of the emerging cultural arts that were uniquely Australian. He made a very short and yet honourable speech about how the Fine Arts in any nation, particularly one coming of age into independence through Federation, gives voice and expression to our unique way of life. Everyone clapped.

Rachel smiled, and leant in to whisper to Cob who stood by her side, "Humph! He scrubs up okay... and talks pretty okay... for a bloke who's a reformed bushranger and a nobody backroom clerk. Who woulda thought he'd visit Shipman Downs?"

Cob smiled at her thick country accent. Squeezed her hand affectionately and whispered back, "And who woulda thought that two smithies from Woop-woop could comfortably partake in an event of such diverting society and culture?"

A number of public figures were quite partial to the story-board approach of the sculpture and made enquiries about commissioning pieces to capture the unique story of their own regional communities. By the end of the day, Rachel had at least three solid contacts for future commissions of substantial community projects. Gwendolyn quickly jumped on that bandwagon and commissioned Rachel to make her a garden bird feeder that would tell her story. Walter was shocked that he had been kept in the dark about Rachel's fascination with iron as an artistic medium. He was even more shocked when there was a live demonstration down at the blacksmithing shop, with Rachel working a simple art piece at the forge, that was to be added to the closing charity auction for disadvantaged children. Blacksmiths are common, but a woman using this as the vehicle for sculpture... one who was even experimenting with the emerging art of welding, that was a curiosity for sure. But on a day like today, with the Bohemian element of the arts being unapologetically displayed, it seemed less controversial.

At the end of the day, the guests dissipated with their artwork; the public left to resume life in the valley; and the staff began the process of pulling down the pavilion. Rachel finished farewelling some art patrons who were insistent on a personal autograph in their keepsake book, and she came over to where Cob stood with his mother. "Thank you so much for coming and making this the most wonderful day," said Rachel, offering her mother-in-law a genuine hug.

"Oh, Rachel, it was our pleasure. We were so disappointed to miss your wedding day." This was something that she mentioned with sadness.

Rachel tilted her head and acknowledged that during all of those wedding preparations, she had not even considered Cob's family. "Tomorrow, would you come for lunch at our home, and I could tell you all about it. We did get a nice portrait or two taken..." Perhaps it was time to unveil the controversy of that story. It seemed she fitted into this family well enough with her own catalogue of defiant and rebellious happenings after all.

Cob raised his brow and smirked. "Ahh, Mum, I can guarantee you will be entertained. That it is quite some story..."

"Oh, I would love to hear all about it. I really would. I have thought that today has been like a substitute reception... a celebration of you becoming part of our family in a more complete way."

Rachel's eyes welled up. She didn't expect such kindness, given the silence she had subjected Cob's mother to, after their wedding. "I hope there will be many more family events... but I trust some of them will not require the public spectacle that today has been. Both have a place, I know... but I like the idea of private as well."

Cob put his arm around her shoulder and squeezed it gently. His mother's face burst into a glorious smile. "Oh, my dear, I am so relieved to hear you say that. To be honest, I find this publicity all a bit exhausting. I know Abby thrives on it, but I prefer a different pace. Now... if you don't mind... I would like to go and pay my respects to Jac... and place some of these flowers that have been used on the tables. Would you come with us, Rachel, to his grave? I'm quite sure I would like to have some gentle company..."

Rachel looked hesitantly at Cob who nodded and offered her his arm. His mother took the other. They walked through the gate, over the paddock, to the station graveyard. "Rachel, I am so grateful for the care you gave my brother at the end. He was a stubborn old coot, and for those who didn't know him well, he had the reputation of being an abrasive sort. It seems strange now, but until Theodore was born, we didn't have much to do with each other. But he loved you, Theodore, like his own, and you had such an uncommon connection."

Cob nodded. "It was Uncle Jac who started calling me Cob. He declared we were partners: both with the name Jacob... Jac and Cob.

I refused to answer to anything else from that time forward. Except for you, Mother, of course!"

"I am so grateful we sent you here when we did. Jac was very straight about not wanting someone interfering, and anyone else he probably would have sent packing."

They walked around the gravestones and Callie knelt before a grave where the grass was trimmed tidily. Rachel placed the flowers from Callie's hand in the jar beside the headstone. Callie looked at it intently. "Oh... this is just beautiful!" she gasped, as she studied the wrought-iron cross, where figures were tumbling down the centre of the cross telling Jac's story.

Rachel nodded. "We made this together. We had never done that before... working a joint project like this. But it gave us a way to grieve, and it helped us find the rhythm of working together."

"You have captured so much of who Jac was... oh! This is so honouring. Thank you... thank you." Tears spilt onto the grass as she knelt there.

Rachel knelt beside her and wrapped her arm around her shoulder. "Smithy Jac opened the world of smithing to me. It was like a beautiful wrought-iron window that allowed me to look into a whole world I never knew existed. He never judged me for being improper, and he always encouraged me to reach higher, do better. He didn't just do that with the way I relate to art, but also people... everything." *Even Cob...* she added silently in her heart.

Callie smiled affectionately. "Yes. Jac was like that." Cob helped his mother to her feet and Rachel lingered kneeling a moment longer.

Rachel brushed the tears from her eyes. Jac had been a master-smith, someone who encouraged her to craft a sculpture of grace... just like Cob said, with all the flaws, and twists, and stains and bends... blending all those elements together to forge an art-piece quite remarkable. She stood to her feet, and linked her arm with her husband, and her other with Callie.

As they walked back to homestead, she sighed with a pensive smile on her lips. Yes, Jac was right. In the end... the real prize may not be the article forged in the heat or on the anvil. But rather it is the grace behind the story, that gives form to the scraps as they are shaped and fashioned together, to become the greatest sculpture of all.

Pioneers of Grace Series

Book 1 - Time of Grace

Abigail is the elegant wife of the most powerful station-owner in the valley. But powerful also means brutish and cruel. To correct her husband's crimes, Abby is drawn into contact with the disgraced lawyer Ruben Davey, hiding in the hills with a band of displaced bushrangers. Will Abby be able to address these injustices and find a way to navigate towards a safer future in the meantime?

Book 2 - Circle of Grace

All her life Hannah had been sensible and sincere. When her humble circumstances lead her to work as the companion for Lady Whitmore, she is confronted with Lady Whitmore's nephew, the most shallow and irresponsible man she has ever met. As their life of privilege collapses around them, will she follow Lady Whitmore and Sebastian to Australia, to explore a new life in exile?

Book 3 - Journey of Grace

Tibby had grand dreams that were very different from the squalor of the textile mill tenements where she grew up. She plotted her escape by taking sponsored passage to the Colony as a bride, but everything on this journey was harder than even she could imagine. Dumped like garbage at the gate of Zachary Logan's place, will it be possible for Tabitha to sew a new life together in this barren wasteland of Australia?

Book 4 - Mask of Grace

Late one night, Martha finds herself at a wayside inn, running from the expectations of her family. To stay in hiding, she works as a scullery maid alongside Simmons, who doesn't just cook, but is a culinary artist. Intrigued by each other's secrets, will they be able to drop their pretence long enough to find their true passions?

Book 5 – Crucible of Grace

Ruth has had more than her fair share of tragedy. When her widowed mother-in-law wants to return to the farming region where her family once thrived, Ruth works as a laundry maid to support them. Can Ruth survive the fire of heartache and prejudice to find a new shape for her life, which might even include the station owner?

#1 The Beachside Cottage

In this offering from Olwyn Harris, we meet the heartbroken and downtrodden Eliza-Beth Perkins. Eliza-Beth is facing the dire consequences of her choices and the possibility of life in the poorhouse. Then she, literally, runs into Jensen Harker. Jensen is facing his own heartbreak at the death of his wife and wants nothing more than to be left alone. But something in Eliza-Beth stirs him to make a rash proposal, thus rescuing her from her predicament. As we follow their journey together, will we see them find the healing they both desperately need?

#2 Petrea Downs

In the 2nd book in this series, we meet Meg. Meg's life has been turned upside-down, with her husband gone, trying to run Petrea Downs by herself, and disaster after disaster at every turn. Thankfully, her neighbour Everett Grossman is always there to help. The final blow comes when a cattle duffer tries to steal her only source of income, gets shot, and has to be nursed back to health in her living room. But, is Ben Harker really the villain he seems? And is Everett really the hero he makes himself out to be?

#3 The Writer's Retreat

The third book in the Homes of Healing trilogy introduces us to Tess, a romance writer, who prides herself on letting her characters tell their own story. When she arrives at Rocky Creek B&B, the run-down stone cottage looks like the perfect place for her to retreat to, not only to write her book, but to escape her past. Join her as she discovers her characters and explores their stories, and finds that God is intent on becoming part of her own story at the same time. As her relationship with the local publican challenges her to stop running, she realises that real life and real love can be messy and complicated. Can she honestly confront the ugly aspects in her own story, so that God can bring them both to a place of healing?

#1 Sapphires of Hope

"There is no way," she thought, "that I am going to use this!" She had desperately searched their cupboards for something, anything that would come close to what she needed for her catering project. She found only this old dilapidated breadbasket that looked like the sort of junk that comes from one of those tacky jumble-sale stalls..."
Andi and Jo are best friends... they do pretty much everything together. So, when Andi has a catering assignment due, and only a tacky old basket to use, Jo helps her pull off the faded decorations, revealing a time-capsule of historical information, and in order to understand what it means, Andi and Jo ask their elderly neighbour to take them to visit the farm where the basket came from. They find themselves dumped back in history at the time of Federation, embroiled in circumstances that nearly cost Andi her life and threatens the livelihood of the people living there. How can they ever hope to keep going when things are spinning out of control?

#2 Rubies of Ambition

In the 2nd book in the Gem of Australia series, we again travel with Andi and Jo back in time. On this adventure, they meet the very beautiful and ambitious actress, Lillian Browning, who is on the run from the federal police. Andi and Jo accompany her back to her hometown, where they find she is not well received. Will Lillian find a balance between the past that calls her and the ambitions that drive her?

#3 Emerald Dreams

In the third instalment of the *Gems of Australia* series, Olwyn Harris brings Australian history to life as she takes us on a journey back to the early days of convict settlement in Australia. Here we, once again, find Andi and Jo learning about Australia's true history, and finding strength in God to help others.

#1: A Spacious Place

In this first instalment of the Guthrie's Lot series, set in the late 1800s, we meet Irvin Guthrie, a practical, no-nonsense man with a sick wife and a small child to care for. When his wife's doctor suggests they move to a warmer climate, he spends everything he has on a property that ends up not being what he expected.

Joanna Grenham has dreams of being a schoolteacher. When an opportunity presents itself, she jumps at the chance, only to find herself given no choice but to care for Irvin's sick wife and child.

Will Irvin and Joanna make the most of their circumstances, or will they forever find life as hard and unyielding as the ground in A Spacious Place.

#2: A Level Path

In the second instalment of the Guthrie's Lot series, it is now the late 1960s. Here we meet Irvin's granddaughter Iris. Iris hungers for excitement and adventure, and she won't find that in Gumleigh, or with the ever-predictable Dave. The last thing she expected was for Dave to follow her across the world to England as she tries to find direction and meaning.

Will Iris finally see through the charismatic, but ultimately selfish, Stan, or will Dave leave England alone and leave Iris to find her own way to A Level Path?

#3: The Crying Tree

In this final episode of the Guthrie's Lot series, the year is now 2010. We meet Mac, who has always been an achiever – a do-er, just like her father. After the death of her mother, she finds that she needs to get away, so she buys a little run-down stone cottage in the middle of nowhere to transform into a creative studio. She is taken by the feel of the place - especially the twisted weeping willow tree behind the house, even though it doesn't fit into her plans anywhere.

Dan spent years growing up on the old Guthrie place, so when the new owner arrives, he is not convinced that he wants to work for this headstrong woman, who is obviously used to getting what she wants, but he feels that it is something he has to do – and only God knows why.

Can Dan and Mac work together to make her dreams into a reality? Will she transform the old Guthrie place, and her life, into something unique and beautiful? And what will become of The Crying Tree.

Matt's Boys of Wattle Creek

When Matthew Lawson's three sons were born, he wrote each of them a letter outlining his hopes and prayers for their futures. When he decided to give up his city job and move to the little town of Wattle Creek, he could never have imagined the effect it would have on his young family. As Matt's boys grow to maturity and find their places in their community, will his dreams and prayers come to fulfilment? Will his boys develop their own faith in the eternal God? And will they each find the kind of love that Matt holds for his beautiful Josie?

Maggie & Minotaur

"For Maggie, the mythical Minotaur represented Romance – half man, half beast. The Minotaur was a monster created from centuries of classical Greek mythology and no normal man could withstand its strength...... Sooner or later she would accept that Theseus, the hero, did not exist. She knew that she would have to battle through the maze of reality and confront it herself...."

Maggie Wick was shipped off to the city and high society life at the age of 12, where she would learn the ways of the rich and marry into a family of influence. What could have caused her sudden return to Henderson's Gap? Can she really settle back into life on the station, with all its diversity and challenges? Will she find fulfilment in her role as provisional schoolteacher? Will she ever figure out the "Captain", the mysterious, intimidating, station manager? When war comes to her little haven and Maggie's world comes crashing down, taking her loved ones and the captain with it, Maggie needs to find a way to survive. Will her faith be enough to protect her, and what of the Captain? Could he really be the Theseus who would do battle with her Minotaur?

The Bush Olympics
The Bush Olympics, written by Olwyn Harris and beautifully illustrated by Shelly Askew, shows us that we don't have to be good at everything to be part of a team. Even sleepy Koala is good at something, and if everyone plays their part, we can all be successful together.